HANGROPE JOURNEY

HANGROPE JOURNEY

Jeff Sadler

Chivers Press • G.K. Hall & Co.
Bath, Avon, England   Thorndike, Maine USA

This Large Print edition is published by Chivers Press, England, and by G.K. Hall & Co., USA.

Published in 1997 in the U.K. by arrangement with Robert Hale Ltd.

Published in 1996 in the U.S. by arrangement with Robert Hale, Ltd.

U.K. Hardcover ISBN 0-7451-4936-9 (Chivers Large Print)
U.K. Softcover   ISBN 0-7451-4947-2 (Camden Large Print)
U.S. Softcover   ISBN 0-7838-1881-5 (Nightingale Collection Edition)

The text of this Large Print edition is unabridged.
Other aspects of the book may vary from the original edition.

Set in 16 pt. New Times Roman.

Printed in Great Britain on acid-free paper.

British Library Cataloguing in Publication Data available

Library of Congress Cataloging-in-Publication Data

Sadler, Geoff, 1943–
    Hangrope journey / Jeff Sadler.
        p. cm.
    ISBN 0–7838–1881–5 (lg. print : sc)
    1. Large type books. I. Title.
[PS3569.A247H36   1996]
813'.54—dc20   96–24251

For Mike Stotter
a new and welcome pilgrim
on these age-old trails

CHAPTER ONE

He sat the black horse in treeshade and built himself a smoke, looking out over the country before him.

Along this stretch of the Pecos Valley the land changed colour, grew itself a greener, lusher coating. Nearside, thick clumps of *grama* and *toboso* studded the flanks of the trail that wound downslope for the bed of the creek. Below it, his keen ears caught the murmur of the shallow stream as it trickled over pebbled sand, snaking a shadowed path between clusters of cottonwood and desert willow. Far side of the creek a second, thicketed slope blazed emerald in the rays of the dying sun. Beyond it the country levelled out again, stretched away unbroken to the limits of sight. A vast, solid wedge of grassland whose tall spears reached almost as high as a horse's belly. Good cattle country, all right. The best a man could hope to find.

Worth killing for, maybe.

He frowned then, not bothering to answer the unspoken question in his mind. Anderson struck the match, cupped it as it spat and flared to life. Last of the sun's heat burned his shoulders, washing the stand of *piñons* higher up the slope with a pattern of bloody stains. The tall man in the buckskins paid it no mind,

1

his gaze intent on the smaller flame he held to the tip of the cigarette. The matchflame lit the harsh, dark features, reflected for an instant in the eyes with their pale, piercing stare. Anderson shook out the dead stub and let it fall, drawing tight-lipped on his smoke as the sun edged lower and a deepening shadow swept over the grassland beyond the creek. So far, he hadn't cared for what he'd been told. Only trouble was, he had the feeling it might just get worse.

Above him a breeze ghosted through the *piñon* branches, set them to moving with a faint, creaking sound. Something in the noise unsettled him and he glanced up sharply, the back hairs starting to prickle on his neck. For a while it was almost as if he glimpsed some unseen shape there, some half-remembered spirit that swayed gently in the depths of his mind, dangling from the boughs that bent and creaked to the tug of the wind. The dark man eased the cigarette from his lips, breathed hard as he exhaled a slow trickle of smoke. Nothing up there to bother him, Anderson decided. Not yet, anyhow.

Hell of a while since he'd been here last, in this part of New Mexico. Then, it had been the throw of a rope, and a hanged man, that had brought him this far north. Pondering on that he frowned harder, drawing afresh on the cigarette. Looked like things could be working out the same, this time around.

2

The rasp of folded paper that shifted against him as he moved brought another reminder. Anderson touched the place where it nestled in the breast pocket of his buckskin hunting shirt, his dark face stony as he savoured the acrid taste of his smoke. No need for him to study the words on the telegram he carried. It had been three days since he'd read them first, back in Severo, but he figured he could remember the message all the same.

Come quickly, Andres, Josefa had written. *They mean to hang Diego.*

Behind him the westering sun dipped lower, shadows darkening on the trail and spreading to cover the far grassland like a black tidal wave. Anderson finished the last of his smoke, pinched out the cigarette butt before flicking it away. He'd made the best time he could to get here, mostly by train before this last stretch on horseback, and hardly a stop between. This was the first real halt he'd allowed himself since leaving Sonora, and he reckoned it would have to be the last. From the way Josefa told it, he might already be too late.

He shook his head angrily, struggling to throw off the unwelcome thought. That was one possibility he couldn't let himself accept, that Diego Galvan was already dead. Still less that his old friend had ended his life the worst way of all, choking for breath with a hemp rope around his neck. Anderson swore softly, his pale eyes cold and murderous in the darkness

3

of his face. Any man who hanged Diego was due to regret the day that he was ever born, and that was a promise.

Dust lifted in the bed of the trail as the stallion fretted under him, ducking its head to drag on the rein. Anderson breathed out more easily, the momentary anger ebbing from his features. The dark man touched heels to the black horse's flanks, man and beast coming out together from the shadow of the trees. Taking the trail downhill through the boulders and grass clumps, Anderson let his right hand settle on the worn butt of the old Colt Single Action Army that lay holstered at his hip, felt the hard, reassuring touch of the Winchester carbine nudge his leg through the leather scabbard. It had been a while since he'd needed to use either one of them, and that was something he didn't regret. The way the land lay now, though, it looked like he might find work for both.

He walked the stallion down the last of the trail where it led into the willows, and forded the shallow creek for the grassland beyond.

By the time he came to the ranch-house it was getting on towards dark, the last faint flush of the sunset vanished and shadows cloaking the land about him as the first stars pricked out overhead. Anderson rode the black horse in beneath the big JD sign that hung above the entrance gate, and along the stone-laid drive that led towards the *hacienda*. The white adobe building loomed palely from the surrounding

4

mass of shadows, slowly taking on a firmer shape as he drew closer. The dark man's glance touched on the pillared stone columns of the verandah, the iron-work balcony and open staircase leading to the upper rooms. The place was just as he recalled it from the last time he'd been here. That time, he'd been moved away at gunpoint. Hopefully he was due for a more friendly reception on his second visit.

A short distance from the house he heard the fierce barking of a dog, and caught sight of figures in front of the *hacienda*. Anderson reined in his mount as the dark shadow-shapes of half-clothed men broke out from the nearby bunkhouse, some of them grabbing for boots and pants as they ran. The yellow gleam of a lantern broke the darkness, and by its light he saw the tall, upright figure of the woman who came to meet him. Close behind her the shorter, crouching shape struggled to hold on to a couple of huge mastiffs as they bayed and fought their leashes. Over the furious noise of the dogs, he heard the woman's voice.

'So, you are come, Andres,' Josefa said.

'Just as soon as I could make it,' he told her.

He held the black still with an effort, keeping both his hands in sight on the reins. Dogs were still barking savagely, and the wakened *vaqueros* had moved in to make a half-circle around him, ringing him with their levelled guns. For the moment, he didn't pay them too much attention, his gaze fixed on the standing

5

figure in front of him. Meeting that look, Josefa Galvan smiled.

'Then you are surely welcome, Andres,' the woman said. She turned to the men who stood with their guns still lined on him, her voice cutting sharply above the barking of the dogs. '*No tiran, hombres!* This one is a friend.'

Behind her the short man spoke curtly to the mastiffs, and the huge beasts sank low to the ground, their baying subsiding to a deeper growling as they eyed Anderson balefully. Around him the encircling bunch of *vaqueros* gave back, lowering the pistols and carbines they held. Josefa didn't move from where she stood, turning once more to face him. This close, he figured she was as tall and striking as the time he'd seen her first. A white high-necked blouse and a long, black riding-skirt sheathed the outline of a full, womanly figure, and the set of her head was firm and proud. Light from the lantern bathed strong, handsome features whose Indian ancestry showed plainly in the broad cheek-bones and the dark depths of the eyes. The thick blue-black hair was drawn back from her face and pinned with a comb, but a single gleaming lock escaped to fall forwards into her eyes. Now she brushed at it, fighting hard to hold on to the smile. As smiles went it wasn't so much, kind of weak and shaky at best, but Anderson sensed the pain and grief it tried to hide, and did his best to return it.

6

'Where is he now, Josefa?' the dark man asked. In an instant, he watched the brave smile vanish.

'*Quien sabe*, Andres?' Her voice was almost a whisper. Anderson caught the sadness in the sound, saw the stricken expression that marred her face. 'It has been almost four days now, and we have had no word.' Abruptly she shook her head, some of the old strength returning. 'You have travelled far to come here, Andres. Best you should come inside, and rest.'

'*Gracias*, Josefa.' Anderson swung a leg and climbed down, wincing a little to the ache of his limbs after hours in the saddle. He handed the halter-rope to the nearest of the waiting *vaqueros*. 'Be obliged if you could see him rubbed down an' watered, feller. The two of us come a ways together.'

'*Naturelmente, señor*.' The Mexican ducked his head gravely, taking the rope from Anderson's hand. He led the black stallion off towards the stables as Anderson followed Josefa and the others back for the doorway of the *hacienda*. Not far behind him he heard the dogs growl softly as their under-sized handler brought them along on the straining leashes. Josefa, too, heard the sound, and halted, looking back to the short *hombre* who followed.

'*Bastante*, Raul,' Josefa told him. This time the weariness showed plain in her voice. 'For now, there is no danger. Feed them, and let

7

them sleep.'

'*Seguro, señora,*' Raul nodded agreement, his wizened features breaking to a wide, gap-toothed grin. Glancing towards the *hombre* in the moment he spoke, Anderson saw him clearly for the first time in the glare of the lantern. Raul was an oldster someplace between fifty-five and seventy, his shrunken rail-thin frame rigged in a scarred brush jacket and rawhide leggings. Lamplight gleamed from his bald skull, tonsured around the sides with grizzled wisps of hair, and his gullied features looked like they'd been cut by a knife out of hickory wood. The veteran sensed Anderson's gaze touch on him, and for an instant the dark man felt his own stare matched by two black, seemingly unfathomable eyes. Then Raul grinned once more, hunching aside in an awkward movement that hitched one shoulder higher than the other as he and the dogs stumbled away into the darkness. Anderson frowned uncertainly, watching until the group of them vanished into the shadows at the far side of the *hacienda*. Beside him, Josefa called out to the dozen or so *vaqueros* who now stood impatiently, shouldering their unfired weapons.

'*Mil gracias, muchachos.*' She forced the briefest of smiles, spreading her hands in an apologetic gesture. 'No trouble, my friends. The Señor Anderson is here to help us. *Buenos noches, hombres.*'

8

From the bunch of half-clad, bleary-eyed *vaqueros* came an answering murmur of '*Buenos noches*.' They turned, heading back for the bunkhouse, their pistols and carbines held at the trail. Anderson and Josefa Galvan stood a while in silence, watching them go.

'You, too, must be tired, Andres,' the tall woman said at last. Hearing that note of concern for him in the midst of her own troubles, Anderson grinned wearily and shook his head.

'I've had worse times, I reckon,' the dark man told her. He took her arm gently, escorting her back to the door of the house. 'Right now I want to hear about Diego, an' just what in hell's been happenin' out here. Rest I kin always catch up on later.'

He stood back to let her by him through the open door, and followed her inside.

* * *

'So tell it from the start, Josefa,' Anderson said. 'I'm listenin'.'

He leaned back in the heavy pinewood chair, one booted foot crossed over the other as he studied the room around him. Like all other rooms in the *hacienda*, the *sala* was laid out in the old Spanish style, with arched doorways and high narrow windows. The dark man scanned the carved wood of the *vigas* that spanned the ceiling overhead, the brightly coloured Navajo rugs and shawls that hung on the walls, the shelves with their range of pottery ornaments and the lamps that glowed yellow through their glass mantles. No doubt about it, Diego and Josefa had found themselves the place to settle down, he thought. As of this minute, fresh from a soak in the tub and with a prime steak inside him, cradling a glass of *vino rojo* in both his hands, Anderson figured he just might get around to feeling at home here himself.

Across from him Josefa Galvan hesitated, her handsome features troubled and unsure. The *hacendada* sat with both hands clenched on her thighs, her tall frame tensed as though awaiting a blow. Anderson didn't move, giving her time, waiting patiently for her to answer. All the same many minutes had dragged by, and the silence was stretched so tight it threatened to snap itself apart, before she spoke at last.

'It is a good place to live, here in New Mexico,' Josefa said. She fought against herself to get the words out, her voice shaking a little as it crossed the space between them. 'The grass here is good for cattle, and we breed a healthy stock, mostly white-face Herefords with some longhorn crosses. We have fifteen experienced hands who can ride and rope with the best. Since you left us here, life has been good to us. For almost five years we were happy here, Diego and me...'

10

She halted a moment, swallowing hard as she fought vainly to speak again.

'All this I know, Josefa.' Anderson's voice, too, was gentler than before. Hearing it, Josefa smiled faintly, some of the tenseness ebbing from her.

'It began six months ago, Andres,' the woman told him. All at once her own voice lost its tightness, grew weary and resigned. 'That was when a man they call Ross Copeland came to Hillsburg, and bought up the old Martinez ranch that borders on our land and that of Teofilo Hernandez to the north. Since that time, there has been nothing but trouble.'

'What kind of trouble, Josefa?'

'*Quien sabe?*' Josefa shrugged, reached hurriedly to brush back the hank of hair that fell across her face. 'At first, the small things. Threats to our *vaqueros* at the line fences, broken fences and straying cattle. Then the offers to buy the ranch, and Teofilo's pasture, and threats when neither of us sold out to him. And after that, much worse things. Our cattle killed and maimed, shots fired from ambush at our men. And then one day our ranch foreman, the *segundo* Arcadio Gomez ... Copeland and his people killed him.'

'An' how'd that happen?' Anderson figured he already knew the answer.

'He was drinking in the saloon in Hillsburg. There was a quarrel,' Josefa Galvan sighed, her features growing a bleak expression. 'It is said

11

that insults were exchanged with one of Copeland's hands, an *hombre* called Mather.'

'Lon Mather?' For once, Anderson sounded impressed. He thought about that for a while, turning the half-emptied glass in his hands. 'Heard of him, all right, but I didn't know he was runnin' loose in these parts.' Glancing again to Josefa, he nodded, 'Reckon I kin tell the rest, huh? They went for their guns, Mather was quicker an' got his shot in first, an' afterwards it was called self-defence. That right?'

'As you say, Andres.' The tall woman shook her head ruefully, both her hands clenching tight as she answered. 'Arcadio was no gunfighter, but he was proud, he would not let an insult pass. They goaded him into fighting, Andres. It was murder, I know it!'

She broke off, the tears welling bright in her eyes as she fought for breath.

'If it was Lon Mather, it was murder right enough. Gomez wouldn't have had a prayer.' Anderson studied the red wine in his glass, his dark face grown harder than before. 'Mather's a gun for hire, one of the best. If your friend Copeland's payin' him, he ain't short of a dollar, I reckon. 'Cause Lon Mather charges high for his services, from what I heard.' He took a sip from the glass, leaned back as the liquor warmed his throat. 'You git yourself another *segundo* then, or were they all too scared to come lookin'?'

12

'We found another, a man called Manuel Espinoza.' Seemed like Josefa hesitated a little over the words this time around, as if she wasn't too happy speaking them aloud. Josefa reached for the drink beside her, swallowed hurriedly before setting it down. 'He heard that we needed a foreman, and came to find us. Diego took him on.' She halted, fighting the tautness in her throat, and shook back the hair from her watering eyes. 'That was the worst of our mistakes, Andres. But for him, none of this would have happened!'

She brushed angrily at her face with the back of a hand, drawing herself erect as she met the dark man's gaze. For a moment the silence came down again, harder than before.

'They killed Espinoza?' Anderson asked, and the tall woman nodded.

'He was found four days ago, in a line shack on JD land.' Josefa had regained her former calm, the words coming from her hollow and without feeling. 'This time it was murder without a doubt, Andres. He had been shot in the back from close range, many times.' For an instant she paused, eyeing him closely. 'They found Diego's pistol nearby, outside the shack. It had been fired, and emptied of its bullets.'

'Uhuh.' Anderson had been waiting to hear something of the kind. Now it came, he knew that it was as bad as he'd figured. 'Reckon I kin remember that pistol, Josefa. He used it when we took on Kingman Booth an' his bunch, last

13

time I was over this way. Griswold an' Grier .44, ain't it? Kind of old-fashioned, an' sure as hell easy to pick out from the rest. An' that was the gun killed Espinoza, *verdad*?'

'They took bullets from the corpse, which fitted,' Josefa nodded, her handsome features troubled. 'There is worse, Andres. Before Espinoza died, earlier that day, Diego had ordered him off our land. There was a terrible quarrel between them, and Diego was angry. He told Espinoza that he would shoot him like a dog if he saw him again. It was a bad thing, all our *vaqueros* heard the threats he made...'

She faltered, the sound of her voice cutting off short. Anderson leaned forward and set down the drink he held, his own face sombre as he studied the woman before him. This minute, it seemed she was finding it hard to meet his eye.

'Has to be a reason, for that kind of a quarrel,' he said at last. 'Diego always did have a short fuse, that's for sure, but some other feller always had to rile him first. Ain't like him to take again a man without he had good cause.' He waited, then, pale eyes probing the uneasy features of the *hacendada*, 'Somethin' you want to tell me about it, maybe?'

Josefa Galvan said nothing, her mouth set tight. The unease in her dark eyes, though, was answer enough.

'Seems like I recall this Espinoza,' Anderson said. His harsh face stayed bare of expression

14

as he spoke. 'Ran into him one time in a gamblin' den in Albuquerque, I reckon. Tall *hombre*, an' a flashy dresser too … Kind of handsome, you might say.'

'He made advances to me, in the absence of my husband!' Josefa flared suddenly into speech, her black eyes fierce on the seated man across from her. The rancher's wife leaned closer to him, her slender body tensing in fury. 'He did not respect me as a woman, or the wife of his employer. Instead he wished to lay hands on me, to make me his mistress, his *puta*!' She drew a shuddering breath and sank into her chair, her hands unclenching slowly. 'Espinoza loved only himself, Andres. He thought himself so handsome that no woman could resist him. Only when I called for the other *vaqueros*, and drew a gun on him, did he leave.' Halting again, she faced Anderson levelly, glints of anger still blazing in the depths of her eyes. 'Have I told you what you wish to know, perhaps?'

'You know I had to hear it, Josefa,' Anderson told her. He hoisted the glass, taking another sip of the wine. 'So you told Diego, an' he gave Espinoza his marchin' orders like you already told me, huh?'

'To be sure. Espinoza was already leaving when Diego found him,' Josefa sighed, the last of the anger ebbing away to reveal the stricken, pained expression beneath. 'Now Diego has gone, and they are hunting him like an animal

15

in the thickets! And when they find him, they will hang him for a murderer. And he is innocent, Andres, I know this!'

She began to sob, hands to her face as her iron resolve gave way at last. The dark man got up from his chair, awkward for a moment in the presence of her grief. Anderson came around behind Josefa Galvan, and laid his hands on her shoulders.

'Take it easy, Josefa.' Above her, his harsh face gentled, the voice losing its hardness. 'No need for you to tell me that. Diego Galvan never yet shot a man in the back, an' at close range there ain't a chance he'd need five slugs to do it.' He stayed there a while, gripping her shoulders until the worst of her weeping subsided and she straightened up, drawing her hands from her face. 'So where's this line shack, an' who found the gun?'

'Three miles to the north, where our land joins with Copeland's,' Josefa answered calmly, blinking the tears from her eyes. 'It was Martin Quiroga, one of our *vaqueros*, who found the body first. Afterwards Raul searched the place with the dogs, and the pistol was found. Later, Copeland's men were there, and the sheriff from Hillsburg.'

'Uhuh.' Anderson gave her shoulders a final, reassuring squeeze, and released his grip, moving around again to face her. 'Tatum Hatch still the sheriff around these parts?'

'That is so,' Josefa's voice held a sad,

16

regretful note. 'He is a good man, Andres, and a friend to us, but what can he do? The gun is Diego's, and the bullets match. What else is he to think, when they are found?'

'No other tracks at all?' Anderson had begun to frown again, pacing the floor.

'None that could be read easily.' Her voice came after him as he stalked the room, bringing him no comfort. 'Noise of the gunshots must have scared the cattle, and they ran. The ground was badly trampled when they found Espinoza.'

'Friend Copeland again, I'll bet,' Anderson bit out the words, feeling his own anger rise. 'Man rich enough to buy a gunhawk like Mather would have all the angles covered, I reckon. An' when a feller gits that big, like as not he ain't satisfied until he has it all.' He came to a halt in front of her, his gaze and hers locking together as she glanced up to him. 'You say he's already made a bid for your place?'

'Many times. Our ranch, and the pasture of Teofilo Hernandez, who holds the water rights.' Josefa nodded, the bitterness returning to her voice. 'He is already the biggest rancher in this part of the country. Now he wishes to become the only one, as you say. And with Diego a hunted criminal, he will be stronger than he was before.'

'Strong enough, with Mather to back him up,' Anderson frowned, scratching at the lank

17

black hair that covered the back of his neck. 'That's one *hombre* I'd walk away from, given the choice, an' I'd be a fool to tell you different.' Abruptly he shrugged, as if to shake the cold thought from him. 'So Diego made a run for it, after the killin'?'

'He would have stayed, when the sheriff came.' Josefa pushed out of her seat and stood to face him, her chin lifted as her eyes blazed with a defiant pride. 'Diego Galvan is no coward, he would have remained here to prove his innocence. It was I who persuaded him to run, Andres. I knew that he could not be the killer of Espinoza, that he was here at the ranch with me when the murder was done. But I knew also that Copeland and his hired men had made him appear guilty to all but myself, and that to stay here would be to put his head in a noose.'

'Yeah.' The dark man let the word come from him like a heavy sigh, nodding agreement. 'Reckon I kin see that, Josefa. Whatever you told the judge, chances are they'd think you were just coverin' up for your husband. Trouble is, he ain't likely to stay free of 'em for long. Hatch an' the others know the country just as well as he does, an' sooner or later they're gonna find him.'

He glanced to where his drink still lay untended, turned from it, and let it lie. Anderson met the dark stare of Josefa Galvan, and felt the words dry up in his throat.

18

'Only you can save us, Andres,' the woman told him. Josefa's eyes searched his face, her low voice pleading with him. 'You saved us before, when Diego was a broken man, a drunkard without honour. Before you came to us, he had become nothing. With you, Diego grew to be a man again, life was good. To lose him now, after all that has been ... it is too much. You must help us, Andres.'

She reached out, seizing his hands in hers. Anderson felt that desperate grasp, heard the emotion that trembled behind her speech, and sighed. He knew now, if he hadn't before, that he had no choice.

'Don't you worry about a thing, Josefa,' he said. 'I aim to do what I can, you hear? They won't hang Galvan, an' that's a promise.'

Josefa didn't answer, gripping his hands tightly as the force of her feelings left her too choked to speak.

The sudden noise of barking and the yelling of voices broke them apart. The night air rang to the sound of hoofbeats, and the slither of horses reined to a halt outside. At once, the baying of the mastiffs took on a louder, more savage, note. Anderson stood back as Josefa loosed her hold, his lean face tightening in a moment.

'Looks like you got visitors,' the dark man said.

She said nothing, already pushing past him as she ran for the door. Anderson spared a final

19

look for the undrunk wine, and lunged after her as all hell broke loose outside. Even as he moved, his right hand edged down to touch the holstered gun-butt on his hip.

Could be he'd be needing it sooner than he thought.

CHAPTER TWO

There were four horsemen out front, sitting their saddles motionless as statues as the dust swirled up around them. Anderson caught sight of them as he stepped out through the entrance door of the *hacienda*. He halted, his right hand still resting on the .45 Colt's cedar butt. In front of him, Josefa stood tall and arrow-straight on the verandah steps, facing the four riders as her *vaqueros* aimed pistol and carbine at these latest visitors, and hunch-shouldered Raul fought to quiet the hounds that bayed and hauled on their leashes.

'No call for shooting, Mrs Galvan,' the nearest of the horsemen said.

He smiled with the words, easing rein to bring the horse a half-step closer to the woman on the verandah. At once the dogs set up to barking fiercer than before, and the armed *vaqueros* tightened the grip on their weapons, some of them glancing towards Josefa as if expecting her to give the order to fire.

20

'No shooting,' Josefa told them.

She stretched out both arms as she spoke, moving them downward in a calming gesture. At the signal the Mexican cowhands scowled and muttered among themselves, but moved to lower their guns. The pair of mastiffs still barked and snarled as Raul bent over them, speaking some unheard words to soothe them to quiet. Out in front of the house, the horseman had reined in his mount again, waiting.

'You are not welcome here, Mr Copeland,' Josefa said. Though she spoke with an icy calmness, Anderson saw the tight, clenched set of her body against the dark, and knew the tension that underlay the words. 'Go from here now, or my *vaqueros* will become angry.'

She bit off the last of the sentence sharply, drawing in her breath, forcing herself to stand straight and meet his look head on. Watching from the doorway, Anderson found himself admiring the courage of the woman all over again. The *hombre* on the horse, though, appeared hardly to notice, smiling still as he ran his gaze over Josefa and the group of men around her.

'I'd scarcely call this neighbourly behaviour, Mrs Galvan.' Ross Copeland was anything but impressive at first sight, thin and undersized, his ungainly frame draped in a black Prince Albert coat and woollen pants that clung awkwardly to his jutting knees and elbows.

21

The dull yellow beam of an upraised lantern showed a narrow, freckled face beneath the shade of his derby hat, with eyes that sent back a mocking amber glint of their own. Now he touched a hand to the derby's brim, the smile spreading like a stain across his pinched, clean-shaven features. 'Just thought I'd pay you one last call, out of politeness shall we say? Name your price, dear lady, and I'll take the property off your hands.'

'The ranch is not for sale, Mr Copeland!' Josefa called out sharply above the raised voices of the *vaqueros*, her hands clenching at her sides. 'And you are not our neighbour, you have not behaved to us as a neighbour would! Take your money, and go from here! We have heard enough!'

'Maybe you oughta hear some more, lady, if you aim to stay healthy,' the second man said.

He and the other two riders didn't move from where they sat their horses, a couple of paces or so behind Copeland. All the same, his voice carried plainly to them. At the sound of that voice, Anderson stepped forward from the doorway, moving to join Josefa on the verandah steps.

'Maybe you ought to learn yourself some manners, *hombre*,' the dark man said.

With his last words the crowded space in front of the house went quiet as a graveyard. Even the dogs quit barking for a moment. In that brief spell of silence the cold stare of

22

Anderson scanned the three riders who now spread out behind Ross Copeland, their bodies grown tense in their saddles. The *hombre* who'd called was new to him, a burly thickset rough in a black, double-breasted shirt and tight, pinstripe pants. The flashy rig seemed at odds with his bearlike build, and the wide dishpan features. The pair on either side of him looked more familiar, a thin pale-faced gunsel and a taller, hard-looking man whose jaw held the dark stain of freshly shaved stubble. The hickory shirt he wore looked to be new, and the last time Anderson had seen him he'd been unshaven, but in spite of the changes he reckoned he knew them both. Right now, though, it was the thickset *hombre* who claimed his attention.

'You talkin' to me, feller?' the black-shirted gunman asked. He made no play for the holstered gun he wore, butt forward on his left hip, leaning on his saddlehorn as he scoured Anderson with hard, untrusting eyes. To left and right of him, the other two had begun to fidget edgily, hands drifting closer to their guns.

'That's right,' Anderson told him. He stood clear of Josefa at the verandah's edge, hand resting easily on the .45 Army's butt. 'Lady here was talkin' to Mr Copeland, an' way I see it she don't need no advice from you.'

Hombre's face was wide and battered, pitted with old scars, its nose flattened and slanting

23

askew. Now the features distorted further, the mouth tightening as the words hit home. The horseman was set to answer when Ross Copeland cut in again.

'I see you have some help, Mrs Galvan.' The little man's smile had thinned by a shade. Copeland studied the tall dark *hombre* on the verandah, taking in the buckskin shirt and faded denims, the weapons belt that circled the waist. He let his glance drift slowly upward to the dark Indian face with its strangely pale eyes, the lank gleaming hair that fell to the *hombre*'s neck from under the old Army hat. 'And who might you be, if it isn't too much to ask?'

'Name's Andrew Anderson.' The dark man didn't smile in answer, his lean face stony hard as he looked the rancher over. 'I was out here once before, Mr Copeland. Ask Fisher an' Hindman back there. They both remember me, I reckon.'

Something in the sound of his voice razored the smile from Copeland's lips. The man in the derby glanced back to the waiting gunhands, and the sullen scowls on two faces were answer enough. Copeland shrugged, turning back again to Anderson.

'Come to think of it, I've heard of you myself.' If the rancher was shaken, he didn't let it show too plain, the sly smile easing back to coat his narrow face. 'You must be the one they call Apache Anderson, the half-breed lawman

24

out of Old Mexico. That right?'

'You could put it that way.' Anderson bit down on a fresh spurt of anger, letting the insult pass. 'Can't say as you look like no rancher to me, Mr Copeland. How come you should be takin' an interest in cow-punchin' at this time of your life?'

'That's my business, breed!' Copeland spoke hurriedly, cutting him short. For a moment the tight smile wavered, then held firm. The little man shook his head, chuckling in his throat. 'Yeah, I heard of you. Old feller in Tucson mentioned your name to me once. Watch out for that Apache Anderson, he's a good man to have for a friend, but one hell of an enemy. That's what he said.'

'Could be he was right.' Anderson's features remained hard and unsmiling. 'Got a friend up here, name of Diego Galvan, Mr Copeland. Anythin' bad happens to him, I git to take it real personal. *Sabe?*'

'A pity you're too late to be of use, Anderson.' Copeland had begun to sound bored, impatient to get the business over. 'Take it from me, your loyalty is misplaced. I have good men working for me, the best. There's no way you'll win against us.'

'Heard tell Lon Mather was on your payroll,' Anderson said.

'That's correct.' The little rancher grinned wolfishly, baring his teeth. 'Lon works for me, one of several useful fellows in my employ. Best

man with a pistol you ever did see, Mr
Anderson.'

'He's good, Copeland.' Anderson fixed the
horseman with a bleak, pale stare as he spoke.
'Maybe I seen better in my time. You tell him
that. Meantime, the lady just asked you an'
your friends to leave. I reckon you better do
like she says.'

'You callin' that bitch a lady, breed?' the
thickset *hombre* shouted.

His voice cut harshly through the quiet,
echoing back from the walls of the house.
Anderson sucked in his breath as the words hit
him like a bucket of icewater, clenching his
teeth. Around him the Mexican *vaqueros* cried
out in fury, some of them lining their guns on
the waiting horsemen. From beside Anderson,
Josefa called out again, her own voice lashing
whiplike through the other sounds.

'*No tiran, muchachos!*' the *hacendada*
warned them. 'No killing here!'

Anderson didn't turn his head, eyes still cold
on the undersized rancher in front of him. As
the cowhands mouthed their smothered curses
and eased their weapons lower, the dark man
spoke again.

'Best tell your dog back there to quit
barkin',' Anderson said. 'If he don't, he's due
for a whippin', I reckon.'

Copeland made no reply, keeping his smile
tight. Behind him the black-shirted rider
leaned over the neck of his mount, yelling to

26

the listening group by the house. 'You aim to try it, come ahead!' the burly *hombre* shouted. 'She ain't nothin' more than a two-bit whore, an' that's a fact! Don't think we ain't heard 'bout what went on between her an' that greaser Espinoza, while her old man was away...'

He broke off suddenly, watching as Anderson unbuckled the gunbelt from his waist and let it fall slowly to the boards by his feet.

'Fisher an' Hindman I already met, Mr Copeland,' the dark man said. From the rancher, his glance went swiftly to where the other bulky figure leaned towards him in the saddle. Rested there, hard and merciless. 'How 'bout you introduce me to your other friend now.'

'Hal Grierson's the name, breed!' the heavy-set rider shouted. All at once a mean, ugly grin broke over his battered face. Catching the words, Anderson nodded.

'That's better,' he told the staring bunch around him. 'Never did care to fight a man I ain't come to know well before I start.'

He stepped down from the shelter of the verandah, into the hard-packed dirt that made a floor in front of the house. Anderson had already begun to walk past Copeland to the other horsemen when the rancher's voice touched on him again.

'I really wouldn't advise it, Mr Anderson,'

27

Ross Copeland told him. The sly, mocking tone behind the words rubbed the dark man rawer than a burr in a blanket. 'Grierson was a prizefighter once. He's killed men with his hands.'

'I'll take my chances,' Anderson said. He didn't look around, still walking steadily on to where the three men sat their horses, smiling now as they waited.

'Andres!' Another, more urgent voice came after him, ringing out against the freshly fallen stillness. 'Andres, do not do this thing, I beg you! He is an animal, you will be killed.'

He heard the fear that tremored in the sound of her voice. Disregarding it, his lean face bleaker than hewn rock as he bunched his hands into fists, going forward.

It's what Diego would have done, if he'd been here, he thought.

Grierson had settled back into his stirrups by the time he reached them, both huge hands rested on the reins that he'd looped around the horn. From down by the side of the horse, Anderson got a good look at those hands, and felt a chill, unpleasant sensation at the pit of his stomach. Seen close, they were massive, with scarred, busted knuckles that held callouses like layers of stone. Anderson drew a long, even breath, and looked up to the wide, grinning face above him.

'Git down here, you son of a bitch,' the dark man said, and Grierson grinned wider, an ugly

28

lopsided grin that threatened to take his face apart.

'Here I come, you half-Injun crowbait,' the thickset *hombre* muttered.

He kicked out as the first words left him, aiming the toe of his boot for the other man's head. Anderson had been expecting the move and countered swiftly, ducking aside as his left hand caught the boot-heel and wedged it into stirrup-iron, heaving both of them forward. Thrown off balance, Hal Grierson yelled and pitched backwards over the crupper of his mount, hitting the ground with a solid, racking thud. For a while he stayed there, grunting and shaking his head as he fought to regain his half-scrambled senses. Anderson walked around the fretting horse and stood back with both his fists cocked, waiting.

Grierson snarled out something that was muffled by the dirt in his mouth, and launched himself up from the ground. Anderson saw those massive fists upraised and grimaced, backing away. He managed to sidestep the first murderous swing, and lined himself up for a vicious right to the other's jaw. The blow smashed Grierson hard on the chin, jolting him backwards for an instant. It was a blow that would have put down most men, but Grierson was hard all the way through. He rocked on his heels, but he didn't go down. Anderson barely had time to register the throbbing in his knuckles before a fist like a hunk of gnarled

29

rock slammed him in the chest and sent him staggering. He was still struggling to stay on his feet when a second punch exploded a fireball on the side of his head, and threw him bodily into the dirt.

'Git up an' take your lickin', Anderson,' the prizefighter called.

He spoke the words thickly, spitting out the blood and dirt from his mouth. The heavy, rasping sound of his breathing came from close above as Anderson groaned and fought to rise, teeth clenched against the pain of his bruised head and chest. He rolled awkwardly from a stamping kick that drove dirt into his eyes, clawed at the other's leg to haul him down. This time Grierson avoided the full impact of the fall, bracing his palms to cushion himself as Anderson rolled away and scrambled upright. The thickset man got quickly to his feet, came in again for Anderson with both huge fists lifted. The dark man had time to measure the size of his enemy as Grierson came towards him, and figured he had to be out-matched. Anderson was six feet and a couple of inches tall, with a powerful, rangy build to him, but Grierson was close under six feet and built wide as a door, and all of it solid muscle. Watching the other's blood-smeared grin as the prizefighter closed in, Anderson decided that he could believe what Copeland had told him. This *hombre* had killed men with his hands, all right.

30

He hoisted both arms up to shield his face and body, and lunged in to meet the oncoming adversary. First punch hammered his shoulder and he felt his arm go numb to the finger-ends, a second blow ripping air close by his head. Anderson grabbed at the prizefighter's belt, dug both heels to swing the other man sideways and around. In the moment that Grierson stumbled clear, he drove with his booted foot for the black-clad *hombre*'s groin. It missed its target, thudding home with bruising force on the inside of Grierson's thigh, and the thickset man drew up with a bitten cry of pain. Anderson shook his hammered arm, gasped aloud as the flow of blood returned, pulsing like fire through his veins. He had steadied himself, waiting as the burly man started in for him once more, when something smashed into the earth between them, throwing a small geyser of dirt to spatter them both. At the cracking report of the carbine, the two men halted, freezing as though turned instantly into stone.

'Enough, *hombres*!' Josefa Galvan had come down from the verandah. Now the tall woman stood with the butt of the carbine braced against her shoulder, muzzle of the weapon trailing smoke as she shifted aim for the smaller, derby-hatted figure of Ross Copeland, fighting to hold rein on his frightened mount some yards away.

'There has been enough death, and enough

31

harm done, Mr Copeland,' Josefa told the rancher. Sound of her voice did not waver, level and threatening as the barrel of the rifle that now fixed on the centre of the rancher's black, watch-hung vest. 'I have told you already to leave my land. If you do not obey me now, be sure that I will shoot.'

'Whatever you say, ma'am.' Copeland smiled easily, quelling his mount with a touch of the rein. Only the tautness of his narrow features gave a hint of what he felt. Now the little man turned his head, glancing at the men behind him. 'OK, Hal. You heard the lady. Let's get out of here.'

Grierson didn't answer his boss, still rubbing the bruised place on his thigh as the words carried to him. The thickset prizefighter sleeved the blood from his torn mouth, raked Anderson with a hard, unpitying stare. For a while, he looked ready to fight again. 'Another time, breed,' Grierson said. 'Just you an' me, an' no woman to pull you out from under. You be ready, you hear?'

Anderson said nothing, grimacing as each breath rasped on the raw, bruised pain of his ribs and chest. He watched as Grierson dug a foot in the stirrup and climbed across his mount, caught the sneering smiles on the faces of Fisher and Hindman to either side. He stayed put, wheezing for breath like a wrecked old man as the three horsemen bunched together, waiting for their leader to rejoin them away from the house. Ross Copeland shook out the rein, the horse stepping almost lazily back towards the three gunhands and their mounts, its rider seemingly unaware of the carbine muzzle levelled on his spine. Some distance from the house the black-coated rancher halted, drawing rein as he spared a parting look for the woman on the verandah.

'Something I almost forgot to mention, Mrs Galvan.' Copeland's voice carried plainly to the listeners in front of the house, making no attempt to disguise its malice. 'I thought it might interest you to know that your husband has been found. Sheriff Hatch and the posse from Hillsburg apprehended him barely an hour ago, the four of us just left them.' Copeland let the smile cut deeper into his thin, fleshless features. 'They'll be on their way back to town with him by now, I shouldn't wonder.'

Stranded halfway out from the house, Anderson stiffened as the shock of the words hit him, freezing into his brain. The dark man glanced towards Josefa, saw her slender body tremble as those same words struck home, hands shaking to bring down the carbine as her face turned white and stunned. From the group of *vaqueros* beside her a young kid burst forward, his pistol lifting for a shot at the distant rancher. Under the brim of his huge cartwheel *sombrero* his smooth face convulsed in rage.

'*Cabron!*' the youngster bellowed after

33

Copeland, struggling to line his weapon as two other Mexicans grabbed him from either side. '*Maricon!* You are not fit to speak his name, *hijo de la gran puta!*'

He fought vainly to break free of the other men, jerking the trigger so the shot blasted harmlessly into the darkness overhead. The young man gave a cry of pain as the pistol was wrestled from his grip. Stood, rubbing angrily at his bruised wrist as his fellow *vaqueros* released him.

'*Silencio*, Martin!' Josefa had regained her voice. The *hacendada* didn't bother to look his way, her eyes still on Copeland as the little horseman smiled and held in his plunging mount. 'I will give you the chance you did not offer my husband, *señor*. Take your men from here, and none of my *vaqueros* will harm you. *Entiende usted?*'

'Much obliged, ma'am.' Copeland touched the tight-rolled brim of his derby in a mocking gesture of respect. 'Just remember you've heard my final offer, Mrs Galvan. When I come here again, it'll be on my terms.'

'When you come here again, it will be over my dead body, *señor*,' Josefa said.

She stood, the carbine lowered in the grip of both hands, watching the four riders turn their horses and head away into the night. Copeland was last to go, his face a pale, smiling blur against the surrounding dark. After a while the outlines of men and horses vanished, swallowed by the night, the faint sound of their hoofbeats fading to silence.

Close to the house the dogs were still growling, crouching low on their haunches. The small, stooping figure of Raul bent over them, murmuring to the beasts as he tried to quieten them both. Anderson took a painful breath and flexed his throbbing arm. He started back for the house, feeling the raw ache of his hammered body jolt him with every step. He gained the space in front of the verandah in time to see the young kid they called Martin crouch down on the ground, scuffling for his gun where it lay in the dirt nearby. Seeing Anderson, the Mexican glanced up uncertainly.

'You'll be Martin Quiroga, *verdad*?' the dark man asked.

'That is so, *señor*.' The youngster regarded him warily, ridding the pistol of its spent shell before sliding the weapon to its holster.

'Was you found Espinoza, right?'

'*Verdad, señor*.' Martin's voice was sullen, resentful. He looked sore and mean, ready to pick up on any insult that offered. 'What is it that you want from me?'

'One favour.' Anderson forced a crooked, pain-wracked grin. 'You reckon you kin bring my horse an' gear from the stables, *amigo*? I aim to ride into Hillsburg.'

'*Seguro*, Señor Anderson.' The kid lost his scowl in a moment, springing up from where he

35

hunkered on the ground. Martin turned, heading for the stables while Anderson picked up his fallen gunbelt and buckled it carefully around his aching body.

'Andres, where are you going?' Up on the porch Josefa Galvan frowned, handing back the carbine to the *vaquero* nearest to her. The dark eyes of the *hacendada* scanned the tall *hombre* in the buckskins, noting the bruised features, the telltale stiffness in his movements. 'What you have just done was brave, but also foolish. *Entiende?*'

'You don't have to tell me that, Josefa,' Anderson grimaced, still flexing his pained right arm. 'Sonofabitch would've bust me apart a minute back.' Meeting her eyes, he grinned again, this time more convincingly. 'That was mighty fine shootin', *amiga. Muchas gracias.*'

'If you follow them to Hillsburg they will kill you,' Josefa told him. Even now, the worry showed plain in her voice. 'Do not risk yourself a second time for us, Andres.'

'It's what I come up here for, ain't it?' the dark man told her. 'Anyhow, they got Diego, an' I reckon he's gonna be needin' his friends. Seems to me I best ride over an' take a look for myself.'

'You will not go to Hillsburg alone.' Josefa spoke with a sudden, fierce determination. In the tawny glare of the lantern her face showed tight-lipped and firm. 'Diego is my husband, I

36

shall not desert him when he needs me most.' Abruptly she rounded on the standing *vaqueros*, calling out, 'Ramon, bring my horse from the stable! Ysidro, choose five men and come with me. We are riding to Hillsburg!'

She started down the steps, holding up her long skirt with one hand to avoid stumbling in the darkness. Catching the questioning glance of the hunch-shouldered Raul beside his dogs, she halted for a moment, and shook her head.

'Not you, *viejo*,' Josefa said. 'Stay here until we return. Someone must guard this place while we are gone.'

'*Señora*.' Raul ducked his head, his expression still one of reluctance. Josefa went by him, walking to meet the *vaqueros* who led out the horses from the stables. Watching that tall, slender figure stalk through the night ahead of him, Anderson all but forgot his own bruised and battered limbs for the moment.

Sure picked yourself one hell of a woman there, Diego, he thought.

He moved stiffly towards the shadowy outline of the stables as Martin emerged, leading the black horse behind him.

CHAPTER THREE

Hillsburg hadn't changed too much from the time he saw it last. In the pale half-light of early

37

morning the town looked as drab and uninviting as ever, the rows of crumbling *adobes* and false-fronts seemingly unaltered where they shored up the sides of the potholed, sun-dried track that was the only road the place could give a name to. At the far end of the street came the plaza and its fountain—still broken, like before—and its paltry cluster of trees. This minute, Anderson didn't pay them too much attention. He was looking at the crowd that had gathered along the nearside boardwalk, and in the street outside the jailhouse. That, and the large number of horses already tethered at the hitchrails, told the dark man all he needed to know.

'The vultures are here before us, *amigos*,' Martin Quiroga said. The bitterness showed darkly in his smooth, boyish features as he spoke.

Anderson didn't answer him, his hard grey stare fixed on the crowd in front. The half-dozen or so in the middle of the street looked to be the normal run of townsfolk, rousing up earlier than usual to catch sight of the killer that the sheriff had just brought in. Among the larger group on the boardwalk, though, he could make out more familiar figures. A thin, sandy-haired *hombre* he knew to be Curt Fisher, and Grierson hulking massively against the saloon wall in his black, double-breasted shirt. Ross Copeland stood near the doors, his long coat hanging loose on the angular frame as he cupped a match to the cigar in the corner of his mouth. Beside him, big Walsh Hindman lounged with one beefy shoulder at the doorpost. The bright checkered shirt he wore, and the loss of his whiskers, were the main changes Anderson had seen so far. Switching his glance to the shingle that fronted the saloon entrance, the dark man saw the legend HINDMAN'S PLACE burned into the wood, and frowned uncertainly.

'It is time to go, Andres,' Josefa Galvan said.

Sound of her voice jolted him from his momentary trance, and the dark man nodded, still frowning. Anderson swung down from the stallion's back, gave the halter-rope to the rider behind him. He waited as the young kid, Martin, helped Josefa to dismount, and took the rein from her hand.

'Señor Anderson and I will go to the jailhouse,' the *hacendada* told the Mexicans, who now sat their horses uneasily, hands close to their sheathed pistols as they eyed the group of men arrayed along the walk. Josefa's gaze raked over the *vaqueros* as the words were spoken, stilling their muttered protests. 'We are here to visit my husband, Diego Galvan, and not to fight wars. If you are fired on, defend youselves, *hombres*. Otherwise, stay here and keep your guns in their holsters until we come back. *Entiende?*'

'*Seguro, señora,*' Martin Quiroga was first to answer, biting his lip. Low murmurs of assent

39

came from the others, and Josefa nodded, some of the hardness thawing from her face.

'*Muy bien, hombres.*' She turned, gathering the long skirt in her hand as she started across the street and towards the jailhouse. 'Do nothing until I return.'

She set off determinedly, striding over the hard-rutted ground. Anderson quickened his own pace, using his longer stride to catch up alongside her. From the bunch on the far boardwalk came a mocking burst of laughter, and the harsh, ugly sound of a voice already familiar to him.

'Chasin' the gals agin, breed?' Hal Grierson shouted from his resting-place by the wall of the saloon. Thinking it over, the dark man decided that the prizefighter looked even uglier when he grinned. 'Ain't too much else you gonna be good for, from what I seen!'

Echoing laughter, and more ribald comments from the men around him, carried to the pair still crossing the street. Hearing the worst of them, Anderson saw Josefa's broad features tighten in sudden anger, and bit down on the urge to answer back. Josefa had been right when she'd told the *vaqueros* not to buy the insults; the last thing he needed now was another run-in with Grierson and his friends.

'Wouldn't be in no hurry, lady!' the thickset gunman called after them. Grierson's flat face threatened to split with the lopsided grin that twisted it askew. 'Galvan's in that jailhouse

40

yonder, an' he ain't comin' out. Not 'til they put the rope around his neck!'

Josefa set her lips tightly together, a pale line blanching along her high cheekbones. She struck her toe against a rut in the dirt and stumbled, almost falling. Anderson moved in to take her arm, his own teeth gritted as more insults followed. He shepherded her across the final yards of potholed street, and to the boardwalk steps. Josefa had begun to climb them when she saw the man who moved to block her way, and halted, pale and tight-faced still as she held herself erect.

'You've come a long way to no good purpose, Mrs Galvan,' Ross Copeland said.

He stood, smiling easily around the cheroot that was thrust in the corner of his mouth, both hands sunk in the pockets of his grey wool pants. Seen in clear daylight, he looked more of a scarecrow than ever, the dusty Prince Albert flapping loose on his undersized frame, the derby hat tugged low to shade his face. This close, Anderson saw that the thin, knifeblade features had an unhealthy yellowish hue, spattered with a clutch of sandy freckles at the cheeks and the bridge of the nose. Under the derby, Copeland's hair was a dark, foxy red, that matched the cold, emerald stare of the eyes. Anderson felt that predatory glance touch on him now, and drew a steadying breath.

'She's here to see her husband, Copeland,'

41

he told the skinny figure above him. 'How 'bout you let us by, an' go mind your business some place else?'

He glimpsed the momentary tremor that caught the other's face, sensed the sudden narrowing of those stony eyes. Then Copeland smiled again, shrugging as he stood aside. 'As you please, Anderson.' The rancher's cold stare flicked over the dark man contemptuously, dismissing him from consideration. 'I doubt that you'll find our friend the sheriff in such an accommodating mood, however. Hatch isn't likely to be impressed by a desperado from Old Mexico, especially when he's the friend of a murderer.'

Beside him, Anderson felt the sharp tug on his arm as Josefa half-turned in fury, all but dragging him after her. The *hacendada* held back her anger with an effort, willing herself to calm again.

'In time, you will be sorry for what you have said, Señor Copeland,' Josefa told him.

She broke away from Anderson in the same moment, sound of her booted feet drumming against the boardwalk as she strode for the jailhouse door. The dark man spared a last, bitter glance for the little rancher, and turned to follow. He'd taken maybe a couple of paces when he caught sight of the tall *hombre* behind Copeland, who now came forward to meet him. Anderson slowed to face the newcomer, aware as he did so that Josefa had halted by the

42

door, and was looking questioningly towards him. For the moment he didn't heed her, meeting the gaze of the man in front.

'*Buenos dias*, Anderson,' the *hombre* said. Hearing the flat, dry lash of his voice, Anderson got the feeling he didn't mean it.

'*Buenos dias*, Mather.'

Lon Mather nodded curtly, standing just out of the dark man's reach. Taller than Anderson by an inch or so, his gangling figure appeared to stoop and fold itself halfway over to avoid the boardwalk roof. The rig he wore was drab and workaday, with a denim shirt and jeans that had faded and worn to a dull, greyish shade. Only the black, tooled leather of the belt around his waist, and the holstered pistol that hung on his right hip, betrayed his calling. Now he studied Anderson carefully, his Stetson-shadowed features sombre and thoughtful.

'Last time I heard, you was in the Indian Nation,' Anderson offered.

'You heard right.' Mather was probably a young man short of thirty, but the lean face was hard and furrowed, cut with weathered lines and crow's-feet around the eyes. Pale, cropped blond hair showed like stubble from beneath the Stetson's brim, and his eyes were a faded, washed-out blue. Their bleached gaze measured Anderson appraisingly as he spoke. 'That was before they told me there was better pickin's out here. *Sabe?*'

43

'I reckon.' Anderson's face, too, was hard and closed. 'Copeland tells me you're on his payroll. That so?'

'Ain't nothin' wrong with your hearin', anyhow.' Mather let his glance shift on to Josefa, still rooted by the jailhouse door. 'She bought your gun, maybe?'

'Diego Galvan is a friend of mine.' The dark man scowled harder, guessing the insult back of the other's words. 'Seems to me he ain't had much of a deal so far, Mather. Could be it's time his luck changed.'

Faintest hint of a smile ghosted across the blond man's lips. The kind of smile you might expect from a dead man, sitting up suddenly in his box to scare the undertaker.

'You got sand, feller, I'll allow,' Lon Mather said. He stroked a gaunt hand over the ivory-butted pistol on his hip, lovingly almost. 'One thing you best remember, an' I don't aim to tell you twice. Go up agin Copeland, an' you answer to me. You hear me good?'

'Ain't nothin' wrong with my hearin', Mather. You already told me that.'

'I'm givin' you good advice, Anderson.' Mather spoke softly, menacingly. 'Just be sure you stick by it, is all.'

'I hear you,' Anderson told him.

Mather eyed him a long moment. Nodded at length, satisfied. The blond gunman edged back around Copeland, and into the group of men on the walk. Anderson caught Josefa's

44

eye, and forced what he hoped was a reassuring smile. He pushed after her along the last stretch, and followed her in through the open door.

'Just what in hell are you doin' here, Anderson?' Tatum Hatch wanted to know.

He swung his booted feet off the spur-scarred desk in the moment they entered, shoving back the chair to scramble upright. Even standing straight, there wasn't too much of Hatch. Barely five feet tall, he looked like he'd been sawn off at the legs some place, although the strength showed in the muscular breadth of his chest and shoulders. More pink scalp gleamed through the thinning yellow-grey hair than Anderson recalled last time around, but otherwise the county sheriff seemed pretty much the same. What bothered Anderson most was the hard, unfriendly glint in those steely-blue eyes, and the grim expression on the normally amiable ruddy features.

'Josefa sent for me. Least I could do was come over, I reckon.' Anderson met the hard stare without flinching, his own voice impatient. 'Figure you might just be pleased to see me, Hatch, us bein' friends an' all, remember?'

'Any other time, maybe,' Hatch sighed wearily, spread large hands in an apologetic gesture. 'Right now you ain't catchin' me at my best, an' that's the truth.' Switching his glance

45

to the woman beside Anderson his expression grew almost rueful. 'Guess you come to see your husband, Josefa?'

'As you say, Sheriff.' Josefa's voice threatened to choke as she answered. The tall woman didn't meet Hatch's eyes, instead looking to the cell at the far side of the room, where the figure of a gaunt, unshaven man stood gripping the steel bars. Sensing the pain behind the words, Hatch nodded awkwardly, turning to lead them over.

'You best come this way, then.' Crossing the room at a short, urgent stride, the little sheriff called out to the lanky redhead leaning by the racked firearms at the far wall. 'Mike, git out there an' clear those *hombres* off the street. Tell 'em there ain't gonna be no hangin' today, an' I'll jail the first man that says different!'

'Sure thing, Sheriff!' Mike Riordan detached himself from the wall, heading for the door. The lanky deputy nodded hurriedly to Josefa and Anderson as he eased by them, ducking into the early morning sunlight. Seemed to Anderson that Mike couldn't get out of this room and the tension that filled it any too quickly. The dark man frowned, dismissing the thought from his mind, and walked with Hatch and Josefa to the barred door of the cell.

'*Buenos dias*, Diego,' Josefa said. This time she couldn't hide the tears in her voice.

'*Buenos dias*, Josefa. It is good to see you.'

46

Diego Galvan murmured the words hoarsely, standing with both big hands grasping the bars of his cell. Anderson ran his gaze over that gaunt, rawboned figure, and felt a surge of mingled pity and rage. Galvan's hair had been grey a while back, but right now he looked old, and the fierce hawkish face thin and hollow-cheeked, the dark eyes circled from lack of sleep. The dark man saw the bruise that shaded one side of the prisoner's face, and swore softly under his breath.

'Come as soon as I could, Diego,' Anderson said. 'Soon as I kin find the proof, we're gonna have you out from here.'

He sensed the impatient movement of the sheriff beside him, paid it no mind. Behind the barred door Diego Galvan chuckled bitterly, shaking his grizzled head. 'You are a good friend always, Andres. For this I thank you.' The Mexican held his gaze a moment, shoulders stooping as though under a heavy burden. 'This time, though, it may not be so easy. It is another time we live in now, my friend. In these days the evil ones go free, and the innocent men are put in cages like animals.'

'Your wife's here to see you, Galvan.' Hatch's brusque tone cut through to them, striking sharply. 'Reckon you oughta say somethin' to her, while you got the chance.'

'I wish to speak with Diego alone,' Josefa said.

47

She looked to the sheriff, her dark eyes appealing. Hatch frowned uncertainly, scratched for an instant at the back of his neck.

'I'm not so sure, Josefa.' The stocky man glanced uneasily to the open door, where Riordan's shouted orders mingled with discontented mutterings from the crowd. 'There's some folks out there wouldn't take it too kind.'

'The hell with them!' Anderson told him. 'She ain't about to slip him a gun or a file, that much I kin vouch for. Now try actin' human for a change, an' let her to him.'

Hatch met that hard grey stare, and sighed again. The sheriff unhooked a bunch of keys from his belt, and fitted the nearest into the lock of the cell door.

'*Gracias*, Andres.' For the first time, Diego Galvan smiled. 'I will not forget this.'

'Just tell me you didn't use that gun on Espinoza,' Anderson said.

'It is the truth, *amigo*.' The gaunt Mexican clasped the bars as the key turned in the lock. 'To be sure, we quarrelled, and I threatened him with death, but he was alive when he left the ranch. The gun was at the *hacienda*, it must have been stolen…'

'That's good enough for me, Diego,' Anderson told him.

He stood back as the door of the cell swung open, and Josefa hurried by him into the dark, cramped room. Turning away as Hatch shut

48

and locked it again, he caught the rush of movement as husband and wife embraced, heard their low, murmuring voices. Anderson went back across the jailhouse and over to the window, its blinds already drawn against the first of the sunlight. Settling himself at the *adobe* wall, he opened his tobacco sack and began to roll a smoke.

'So where's this gun they found?' he asked.

Perching awkwardly on the edge of his desk with both feet clear of the ground, Tatum Hatch frowned and reached behind him. 'It's his, all right.' The sheriff held up the brass-plated Griswold and Grier .44 by its trigger guard, his ruddy face wearily resigned. 'All five slugs emptied, an' they checked with the bullets we found in Espinoza.' He turned, still balancing precariously to set the weapon down on the desk once more. 'Maybe what he says is good enough for you, feller, but it ain't goin' to convince no judge an' jury. Let's face it, he's the one with the motive, threatened the guy in front of witnesses, an' it's his pistol.' Hatch turned back to face the dark man, spreading his beefy hands. 'Look at it any way you want, it's bad.'

'Diego was a gunfighter once, one of the best.' Anderson shook out tobacco shreds into the paper, firmed it expertly to a rolled cigarette, stowed the tobacco sack, and struck a match to light his smoke. 'He don't shoot no one in the back, Hatch, an' you know it. An' he

49

don't need five bullets, neither.' Shaking out the match and letting it fall, he paused, his look questioning. 'Josefa tells me Martin Quiroga found the body, an' then Raul come along. That right?'

'That's what I heard, Martin Quiroga an' Raul Nunez.' Hatch braced both hands on the rim of the desk, his round face frowning gloomily. 'By the time we showed up we had Copeland an' his bunch with us, an' the cattle an' horses had trampled up the place so bad you couldn't read the tracks. Neither Martin nor Raul were too happy about what they told us, but they figured they should give it to us straight. Way they saw it, if they tried to cover up they'd be accomplices at best.'

'Uhuh.' Anderson drew on the cigarette and breathed out the smoke slowly, trying to ignore the aches and pains of his bruised frame where it rubbed against the wall. 'Me, I figure Copeland's into this deeper than he cares to admit. Could be I'll prove it, given time.'

'Reckon you're gonna have to work fast, Anderson.' Hatch's features were gloomier yet. 'Could be I'll be out of a job myself before the month's out. County sheriff's post is set for re-election, an' Copeland has somebody else in mind.'

'An' who in hell might that be?' Anderson began. Halfway through the sentence the answer came to him, and he shook his head, staring in disbelief. 'Walsh Hindman? You

50

surely got to be kiddin'?'

'He was town constable in Galesboro, one time.'

'Damn right he was! Sonofabitch did his best to get me killed!' Anderson scowled at the memory, drawing afresh on his smoke. 'Ain't no way Hindman knows how to use a gun; he couldn't keep order in the goddamn whorehouse. Who's gonna vote him in?'

'Copeland owns a lot of people in these parts,' Hatch told him. 'You see the saloon Hindman owns, back along the street? Copeland got him that. Maybe he aims to go one further, this time around.'

'An' now he has gunhawks like Lon Mather, an' roughs like Grierson on his payroll.' The dark man breathed a new smoke-trail, still frowning. 'Curt Fisher's with him, too, that used to work for Kingman Booth. *Hombre* has money, sure enough, but he don't look like no rancher to me. Just where did he show up from, Hatch?'

'St Louis was what I heard. He works for some big land syndicate back in Chicago.' The stocky sheriff shoved himself off the desk, landing unsteadily in front of it. 'Galvan's right, Anderson. It ain't like it was in the old days, ain't even the same as when Booth was around. Man's good name don't count for nothin', nor how long he's been in New Mexico. Money runs this country, feller, an' the kind of influence that money buys. From

51

what I seen, it kin buy just about anythin' you care to mention.'

'Ain't bought me yet, an' that's a promise.' Anderson smoked the cigarette, his lean face grown vicious. 'I'm up here on account of a friend, an' I ain't through yet. If Copeland an' his pals reckon on hangin' Diego, I aim to disappoint them. Where'd you find him, anyhow?'

'Out beyond Galesboro, into the brush.' Hatch sounded tired. 'Figured he was makin' for Octavio Robles' place, away from Hillsburg an' where we'd think of lookin' first. He didn't come quiet, neither. Took a swipe at Grierson, an' the big son knocked him down. Wasn't nothin' I could do about it.'

'Yeah.' Anderson smoked on, his grey eyes harder than flint above the glow of the cigarette. 'Grierson I already met, an' he's one hard bastard, all right. Wouldn't care to mix it with him, nor with Lon Mather neither.' He sighed ruefully, flexing his rangy body painfully against the wall. 'Looks like I might have to do both before I'm through, maybe.'

'I didn't hear that, Anderson.' All at once the voice of the sheriff grew testy and impatient. Hatch stepped in closer towards the tall man, his round face returning to its former grim expression. 'You got any sense, you won't try it, neither.'

'You know me, Mister Hatch. I never was one to bend the law, not most times anyhow.'

Anderson smoked down the last of his cigarette, crushed out the stub under his heel, then half-opened the window blinds, peering through on to the street outside. 'How long you reckon we got before he goes to trial?'

Out on the street, the crowd had drifted away, Mike Riordan shepherding off the last few stragglers towards Hindman's saloon along the walk. By now the sun blasted the open ground, glaring back from busted cans and wet trash in the alleyways, raising a shimmer of heat from the ruts and potholes. Light dazzled from the glass-fronted door across the street; some kind of office, from the look of it. Shifting his gaze, Anderson saw the scarecrow figure of Ross Copeland step down from the walk, crossing the street in the direction of that burst of light. A taller, heavier man walked with him, the cut of his rig contrasting favourably with that of the rancher. Big, florid-faced *hombre* in a dark broadcloth coat and flowered silk vest, his hair slicked almost flat to his head with a liberal dosing of pomade. Studying the pair of them from his vantage point at the window, Anderson sucked in his breath sharply, hearing Hatch's voice in the room as though it came from a hundred miles away.

'He'll be in court inside a couple of weeks, I reckon,' the sheriff was saying. 'That's always supposin' we got ourselves a judge by then. Old Judge Garvey upped an' died last month, an' right now we're lookin' for a replacement.'

'That's Rutherford out there, with Copeland.' Anderson sounded as if he didn't believe his own words. His stunned gaze followed the two men as they gained the far side of the street, saw the glare of reflected sunlight vanish and suddenly return as the office door closed behind him. 'Last time I saw him, he was doin' his best to git me hung in court.'

'Figured you might remember him.' Hatch's tone held a wry, bitter humour. 'Came here maybe five months back, set up in business as a lawyer not long after Copeland bought the old Martinez place. Since then, they've been mighty close. Could be friend Copeland has his own judge in mind, same as a sheriff. That'd just about see him right, huh?'

'Yeah.' Anderson closed the blinds, stepping away from the window. 'Now I heard it all, I reckon.'

'Señor Hatch!' Sound of the woman's voice broke through the sombre thoughts, carrying to both men across the room. 'Señor Hatch, I am ready to leave now.'

Josefa Galvan stood waiting by the door of the cell, looking towards them. The face of the *hacendada* was paler than before, and there were tear-streaks on her cheeks, but she held herself straight and tall, both hands by her sides. Diego had placed himself a short distance behind her, as if already acknowledging the space between them. His hawkish features, too, were pale and strained, the deep-set eyes dull with weariness. He said nothing, watching in silence as Hatch unlocked the door and Josefa stepped out into the room.

'I thank you, Mr Hatch.' Josefa's voice shook. Closer to her, Anderson saw the brimming eyes, the dark wet smudges on her cheeks. The tall man bit on his lip, feeling his anger returning. Then her glance touched him, and he forgot how he felt. 'You will oblige me by taking me back now, Andres.'

'Sure, Josefa.' Anderson touched his hatbrim dutifully, moved to take her arm. Heading for the door, he called back to the man in the cell. 'Just stay fighting, *amigo*. Gonna have you out of there, that's a promise.'

'*Vaya con Dios*, Josefa,' Galvan said.

'*Vaya con Dios*, Diego.' Josefa choked on the words, one hand covering her face.

Hearing her sobs as he helped her out through the open doorway, Anderson frowned harder. Right now, the dark man was more troubled than he had been before. He'd known he was in for a tough time getting Diego out of that hangman's noose. Now Hatch had shown him the size of the problem he faced, and the more he thought about it, the worse it looked.

He was still frowning as he escorted Josefa across the street and back to where the Mexican *vaqueros* waited, their hands lying close to their undrawn handguns.

CHAPTER FOUR

The line shack broke into sight no more than twenty or thirty yards ahead of him, topping the gentle rise in the ground. Framed against the skyline, it seemed to lean away from the wind that feathered the tall grama grasses along the slope, stooping like a broken-down old man beneath a load. Anderson saw the building in the moment he left the trees, and reined the black stallion to a slower pace. He rode on by until he reached the lip of the rise, looking over. Beyond the summit, the country swept down to a vast expanse of grassland. Scanning to distance, the dark man saw the brown, white-faced shapes of browsing Herefords in the mass of green, the ragged outline of the barb-wire fence that separated the JD from Copeland's Red Rowel spread. Further off, more grazing herds dotted the endless sea of grass, green turning bluish-grey and shadowy as the eyes gave out. Anderson sat his mount a while in silence, listening to the sound of the wind in the grama along the rim. Pretty soon he turned the black with a touch on the rein, heading back for the shack itself.

Seen close, the place looked like it had known better days. Weathered slats had begun to warp loose from the roof, one busted piece hanging to rattle in the wind. The dark man spared a glance for the rusted nails in the wood, the caulking dry and bubbled in the joins. He swung down from the big horse, dropped the rope to leave the animal ground-hitched for the moment. Anderson left the stallion standing and went forward, stepping cautiously on moccasined feet. He'd left his boots back at the *hacienda* when he'd first set out. Way he saw it, they weren't what he needed for the job in hand.

Ground in front of the shack was trampled and churned, the lifted earth hardening to rutted trenches that he had to skirt around. Anderson dropped to one knee, peering closely at the tangled, half-erased outlines of tracks in the dirt. Frowned, shaking his head. Maybe a full-blood Apache or Comanche could make some sense of it, but he knew when he was licked. Any answers he was likely to find would have to come from some place else. He got to his feet carefully, and eased the shack door open to duck inside.

The musty, confined smell of the place hit him first, scent of old blankets and leather harness and the warm, smothering dark. Anderson shoved the door wider to let in the light, bending to study the sign on the floor. They'd cleaned the place up the best they could, but the beaten earth still held a dry, dark stain where the body had been found. Anderson's grey, intent gaze raked the far corners of the room where shadow lay deepest, scoured the walls and low ceiling for any hint of a clue. Not a thing answered, the dark shack interior holding to its secrets. The tall *hombre* in the buckskins breathed out heavily, thumbed the old Army hat back on his head. He'd allowed himself a few hours sleep before coming out here, knowing as he did the need to miss nothing that might show itself. Right now, nothing was all he'd managed to find.

Thought came to him, of the gun lying here. The .44 Griswold and Grier, that had killed Manuel Espinoza. The weapon he'd seen in Hatch's office only hours ago. Anderson frowned harder, crouching with his fingertips resting lightly on the beaten dirt floor. Had to be stolen, the dark man told himself. Diego had nursed that pistol over the years like a man in love, and there was no way he'd leave it lying by the *segundo*'s body, to be found by the first rider who happened along. Somebody else had lifted the gun from the house, like he claimed.

Outside the shack he caught the shiver of movement as the black horse moved from one foot to the other. Anderson glanced sharply over his shoulder, but no further movement answered but the sighing of grasses in the wind. The tall man scowled, one hand stroking thoughtfully at his newly shaved jaw. If it was a theft from the house, that had to cut down the odds, he figured. Most of the *vaqueros* hardly got inside the place, only the closest and most trusted hands would be admitted regularly enough to work out where the pistol was kept. And that left Anderson with some unpleasant ideas that he'd as soon hadn't come to him at all.

He thought about the men who'd been first to the line shack after the killing, the ones who'd discovered the body of Espinoza and the pistol beside it. The ones who'd talked to Hatch, and whose evidence could put a hempen noose round Diego's neck. The youngster, Martin, and the older, hunch-shouldered *hombre* with his twin mastiffs on their leashes. Anderson whistled softly through his teeth, studying the face of each man in his mind. Could have been either one of them, he figured. Both were pretty close to Josefa, from what he'd seen, and chances were they'd be regular visitors to the house for their instructions. Nothing to stop the old man or the kid from lifting that weapon, and gunning down the foreman once they were out of sight. Anderson didn't need to look too hard to see the way Martin felt about his boss, and right now he had no way of telling what Raul Nunez thought. Maybe they'd both seen Espinoza as a rival, a handsome, cocky intruder who had to be disposed of. Martin would have been jealous, for sure, and likely to fly off the handle. No doubt about it, either one of them could have done the killing. Jealousy would have been a powerful motive—maybe, like Espinoza, both Martin and Raul had designs

59

on Josefa themselves—they were in easy reach of the murder weapon, and both had been on the scene before anyone else. Looked at in that way, it fitted.

Anderson shook his head, frowning as he stood straight. That was the trouble, he told himself. Somehow, none of this quite fitted. Given the way it looked, there was still something else he hadn't figured yet, something more important than what he'd already learned. Right now it was no more than a vague, uneasy feeling that wouldn't leave him alone, but he'd grown to trust instincts of that kind. Something about this murder didn't add up, and maybe the answers weren't here in the line shack.

He was still thinking it over when he heard the horse blow fiercely down its nostrils, and turned his head to look again. The black stallion had shifted halfway around, ears pricked as it watched alertly for some unseen thing hidden by the curve of the slope behind them. An instant later the harsh bark of a dog cut through the sighing of the wind, and after it the lower sound of a man's voice. Anderson laid a hand on the cedar butt of the .45 Army in its holster by his side. He stepped out from the shack as the figure of a man on horseback swept out of the fold in the ground and into sight, the pair of huge dogs running before him.

'*Buenos dias*, Raul!' Anderson called.

60

He stood framed in the shack entrance, letting go his grip on the holstered gun, smiling as the two baying dogs plunged in towards him. Seeing him, the little man scowled and reined in his amount, shouting angrily to the unleashed mastiffs ahead, '*Aqui*, Cristobal! Mateo! *Abajo, muy pronto!*'

Whiplash sound of the voice halted the bounding dogs just short of Anderson, the barking easing down to a low, untrusting growl. Both huge dogs sank on their haunches in the grass, one to each side of the man in the shack doorway. Aware of their fierce, intent gaze as it fixed upon him, the dark man found time to be thankful he hadn't tried drawing the gun. Up on the snorting bay gelding he rode, Raul still frowned, his ancient, gullied face hard and wary beneath the shade of his wide-brimmed *sombrero*.

'Señor Anderson.' The oldster ducked his head curtly, black stare holding stonily on the man in front. Raul hitched the collar of the old leather brush jacket higher on his misshapen, upthrust right shoulder, the frown still clouding his features. 'What is it you are doing here, if it is not too much to ask?'

'Thought I'd take a look around the shack. Figured maybe I'd find somethin' the others overlooked.' Anderson met the horseman's gaze head-on, his own flint-eyed stare probing the frail, undersized figure above him. 'What's the matter anyhow, Raul? It's a free country,

61

ain't it?'

Off to the side nearest of the mastiffs growled from deep in its throat, and the dark man fell quiet. Sensing his unease, Raul Nunez smiled for the first time, a sudden puckering of the lips that creased the wrinkled leather of his face.

'To some, perhaps.' The Mexican shrugged, his black eyes glinting slyly at their depths. 'That is for them to know, *señor*. All I can tell you is that you waste your time here, Señor Anderson. I searched this place with the dogs, after the body was found. You will find nothing, be sure.'

'Could be you're right,' the dark man allowed. Anderson stole a wary glance at the mastiffs who still lay watching him from either side, let it come back slowly to the hunch-shouldered rider in front. 'Reckon you didn't care too much for this Espinoza feller, Raul. That right?'

'That is no concern of yours, *hombre!*' At once the leathery smile was gone, the dry gullied features set hard in anger. Raul leaned forward in the saddle, his rail-thin body shaking to hold in its rage. 'You meddle where you are not welcome, Anderson, and I would advise you to go no further. Enough to tell you that Espinoza deserved his death! The *señora* was well rid of him!'

'Now just what in hell do you mean by that...' Anderson began.

Low, threatening growl of the dogs in the grass warned him, cut his sentence short. Anderson glanced up into the black, murderous eyes of Raul Nunez, and drew a steadying breath. 'What I do here is for the *señora*, Raul,' he told the furious Mexican, who now gripped both hands on his saddlehorn, his thin mouth set tight. 'It was her asked me out here, an' I reckon she had my promise. Anythin' I kin do to help her, that's the way it's gonna be.' Seeing no change in the oldster's face, he shrugged resignedly. 'OK, feller, have it your way. Guess I was just leavin' anyhow.'

He turned aside from the man on the bay, moving back to where the black stallion fidgeted at its trailing rope, made uneasy by the dogs and their growling. Anderson gathered the halter, murmured soothingly to the horse as he patted its muscled neck. Behind him he caught the sharp command of Raul, ordering the mastiffs to quiet down. The dark man set a moccasined foot to the stirrup, climbing aboard. He turned the big stallion around, man and horse heading back the way they had come. Raul didn't bother to look towards them as they went past him at a walk, his withered crab-apple face still tight and hard. One of the dogs barked half-heartedly after them, but that was all. Pretty soon they were down into the fold, the wall of the slope cutting Raul and his animals from view, and the only sounds were

63

the soft thud of the stallion's hooves and the whisper of breeze through the tall grama grasses. Sitting his mount, eyes scouring the country about him, Anderson scratched irritably at the lank hair on his neck. He'd barely been halfway through the search when Raul and the dogs had interrupted him. Be damned if he was finished looking yet!

Once out of sight, he swung the black horse away to the right, making for the belt of timber that followed the slope uphill on its far side. Anderson rode into the trees and drew rein in the first patch of shade that offered. Sparse stands of oak and yellow pine broke up the sunlight to bladed shafts that struck in through gaps between the boughs, falling in dappled pools on the grass tussocks underfoot. The dark man studied the narrow stretch of woodland, frowning thoughtfully. Could be he had it wrong, but he figured there was no harm in trying. He set the horse forward, slowing the animal to a gradual, deliberate walk, his grey eyes raking the trees and the ground between as he rode.

Close to an hour had passed, and he'd quartered a sizeable stretch of timber, going back and forth to scour the place for sign, when he found what he was looking for. Higher upslope, in an open space between the trees, Anderson's keen eyes picked out the smear of brushed earth where no grass grew. The tall man rode over and got down from the horse, studying the sign more closely. Smiled coldly, nodding in recognition. Someone had dragged a dead tree limb across this stretch, aiming to rub out the tracks in the ground. Trouble was, they hadn't done too good a job, and the smothered prints showed through. Faint outlines, sure, but plain enough for Anderson to read. Hoofmarks of three horses, moving in single file towards the edge of the trees. The tracks of the middle animal went deeper into the ground in places, as if it carried more weight than the critters in front and behind.

Harsh scream of a jay echoed through the timber, and the dark man shivered to the sound. Anderson got to his feet and mounted up, scanning the ground near the wood's edge for sign. He found bruised half-circles on the grass tussocks here and there, from the same hooves whose prints he'd already seen. Anderson turned the stallion back deeper into the wood, skirting the open stretch where the smeared patch showed and rejoining the tracks on the other side. The sign was harder to follow in the grassy tree-shade, but this time he knew what he wanted to find. He came on a dead tree limb in among the pines, its leafy branches scraped and broken from where it had been hauled along the ground. Fresh hoofmarks came into sight a few yards further on, the middle horse loaded heavier than the other two. The dark fleck of a stain marked a tree bole alongside, and Anderson leaned over, rubbing at it with his finger-end. The tall man touched the finger to his lips. Grimaced, drawing it away. Anderson puckered and spat, wiped his mouth with the back of his hand. What he'd just tasted was the unmistakable tang of dried blood, brushed on to the tree by something passing by. Could have been a wounded animal, or a cut on a horseman's hand. Somehow, he didn't think it was either one.

Up ahead came a small half-circle of yellow pines that all but shut off the trail from sight. Anderson halted there, dismounting to study the ground. This time the tracks were plainer than before. Three horses standing, probably roped to one of the pine-boles nearby. And deeper into tree-shade, the prints of three men, grouped close together. Anderson knelt down, peering hard at the marks in the shadowed dirt. Once you looked closely at a boot-print, it wasn't too hard to tell them apart. Nearest to him had a sharp heel-mark that told him the heel was high, like a horseman might wear. Far side was a flatter, low-heeled type, townsman's boot he figured. Feller in the middle wore high-heeled rider's boots, and big Spanish-style rowelled spurs that left a mark of their own. From the size and depth of the prints, Anderson calculated that the *hombre* with the spurs and the low-heeled guy on his far side had both been tall and strongly built, while the one nearest to him was most likely a smaller man. And chances were they hadn't been here discussing the state of the nation.

Confirmation of his last thought came with sight of more boot-prints that crossed each other in a crazy, tangled mass to churn up the ground. In the middle of it all, a man-sized stretch of earth had been flattened and hurriedly smoothed over. Dark, tell-tale stains had soaked into the ground, blending with the shadows, but Anderson figured he didn't need to look any closer. Right now, he reckoned he had the picture. Feller with the spurs was Espinoza, and the three of them must have met here by arrangement. The small *hombre* had kept him talking while the big man in the low-heeled boots did the shooting, the noise probably muffled by the Mexican's clothing and the surrounding trees. Afterwards, they'd loaded him on to the middle horse, and dumped the body in the line shack, ready to be found. Anderson sucked in his breath, let it go slowly through clenched teeth. He reckoned he knew now who he had in mind.

One question stayed unanswered. How had the bastards come by Diego's pistol? Who was the traitor who'd brought the weapon to them?

He frowned at that, turned away to scour the rest of the ground by the pines. That would have to wait for the moment, he decided. Until he had all the answers, he couldn't say for sure. What he did know was that Espinoza had been murdered here, and the prints of his killers didn't match those of Raul or Martin.

The roots of one of the trees hid a mound of dirt, leaves and broken twigs packed close to hide something from view. Digging into the mess, he uncovered five spent cartridge cases, some of them crushed hastily underfoot. Anderson eyed his new-found treasure thoughtfully and straightened upright, crossing to the waiting horse. He stowed the cartridge remnants in his saddle-bags and grabbed the halter-rope to mount up again. The dark man took the stallion out from the half-circle of pines, and deeper into the last stretch of timber. Way things were, he reckoned he'd found all he was likely to, but maybe he'd uncover a few more secrets if he got lucky.

He was clear of the pines, crossing another open span between the trees, when the cold voice halted him.

'Just look what we got here, boys,' Hal Grierson said.

He came out from the far side of the clearing, his burly black-clad figure outlined plainly against the trees. The thickset man nudged his horse in closer, his pistol already lined on Anderson's belly. Anderson had his own weapon half-drawn when Grierson first called out. Sight of the other two riders, emerging out of the timber to left and right of their leader with their own guns levelled was enough to decide him against it. Anderson let the unfired

Colt slip back into the holster and loosed his hold, keeping both hands lifted in view of the three *hombres* who now moved in towards him.

'Suppose you git down from your horse, breed.' Grierson couldn't hide the sneer in his voice. From the vicious grin that split his dishpan face, Anderson guessed that the prizefighter was beginning to enjoy himself. The dark man shrugged tiredly and kicked from his stirrups, dismounted to stand beside the fretting stallion as the other two got down to join him and Grierson kept him covered. Anderson sized up the opposition either side of him, and knew they had him treed. Thin, pale-featured Curt Fisher stood to his left, cold-eyed and unforgiving behind the levelled gun. To the right was a gunhawk Anderson hadn't met before, a short barrel-chested *hombre* with dark muddy eyes and a thick jet-black beard shrouding the lower half of his face. He too held a pistol, a Remington Army model by the look of it, and the muzzle of the weapon was lined up neatly for a shot at the tall man's middle. Anderson breathed out slowly, his shoulders slumping as the tension went from him. He stayed put, still holding the horse by its halter-rope as Hal Grierson swung down from the saddle to face him. 'So tell us what you're doin' out here, Anderson,' the blackshirted gunman said.

He sheathed his own gun as the words were spoken, taking a step closer as he rubbed his big, scarred hands together. Remembering the power of those fists, Anderson swallowed, willing himself not to move. Away to the side, he caught the mean, thin-lipped smile that broke across Curt Fisher's narrow face.

'Could ask you the same question, Grierson.' He hoped the tightness didn't show too plainly in his voice. 'We're on JD land out here, ain't we?'

'That what they told you, feller?' Grierson tapped one massive fist against the palm of the other hand, the ugly grin turning his face lopsided as he came closer still. 'Let me tell you somethin', breed. Fact is, this ain't gonna be JD land for much longer, you hear? An' we're askin' the questions, so you best answer up. *Sabe?*'

'I hear you,' Anderson told him. Scanning the hard faces and levelled guns on either side, he shrugged again, forcing a phoney smile. 'Just takin' a pasear round the place before I head back south, is all. Diego's in jail, an' it don't look like there's too much I kin do about it. Reckon I'll be makin' for the Rio come the mornin'.'

'Yeah?' Thrown by the tall man's answer Grierson frowned, uncertain for the moment. 'Is that a fact, now?'

'That's where I'm headed, soon as I kin make it.'

'Don't let him fool you, Hal!' Fisher shouted. The thin-featured gunhand pushed in

70

towards Anderson, freckles standing out darkly on his pale, tight-lipped face as rage threatened to overwhelm him. 'I been in with that half-Injun bastard before, an' he's slippery as they come. Let's finish the job here, an' have done with him!'

'Shut up, Curt!' Grierson didn't turn his head, his voice cutting sharply in answer. Force of the words lashed Fisher to quiet, the sandy-haired *hombre* scowling sullenly as he eyed Anderson from behind the gun. Grierson appeared not to notice, the uneven grin still breaking his flattened face. 'No call for gunplay here, I reckon. We just gonna give Mister Anderson a sendin'-off present. Kind of a keepsake to remember us by. Ain't that right, Anderson?'

'If you say so.' Anderson's gaze met the other man's without flinching. Inwardly he groaned, guessing what he had coming. The tall man glanced sidelong to the silent, bearded gunhawk on his right. 'Fisher I met a while back. You ain't introduced me to your other friend.'

'That's right, I ain't.' Grierson eyed the sombre, hard-faced man alongside, and chuckled, shaking his head. 'Guess I forgot how keen you was on introductions, feller. This here's Nathan Coe, a business acquaintance. He works for Mister Copeland same as Curt an' me.' He glanced to the bearded *hombre*, his grin cracking wider. 'Say

71

hello to our visitor, Nate.'

The short gunhawk frowned, growling something from the depths of his beard that Anderson didn't catch. Somehow, he didn't think it mattered.

'Now we're done introducin' ourselves, there's this here other matter to settle.' The burly, thickset figure was within a few feet of him now, the grin suddenly vanishing as though it had never been. 'You an' me got unfinished business, Anderson, an' I aim to take care of it 'fore you ride out of here. Unbuckle the gunbelt, *pronto!*'

'Ain't no need for this, Grierson...' Anderson began. Sight of those hard, malicious eyes stopped him halfway through his sentence, and he went quiet.

'That's just where you're wrong, feller,' Grierson told him. The bulky, hard-muscled prizefighter had regained the smile, starting to duck and weave as he shadow-boxed with both massive fists. 'There's more than one of us here that owes you, Anderson. Curt here, for instance. He'd like first try at you himself, ain't that right, Curt?'

'You bet it is!' Fisher's voice still shook with fury, his pallid features hard and bitter behind the gun. 'You put me away last time you was in New Mexico, Anderson. Five years in a stinkin' jail, once my shoulder healed. I aim to kill you for that!'

'Another time, maybe.' Grierson had begun

72

to sound impatient. 'Right now it's my turn, Anderson. Slack off that belt, an' make it fast!'

Conscious of the two pistols trained on him, Anderson complied. He was halfway through loosing off the belt when Grierson came at him with both fists up and ready. He moved with startling speed for a man of his size and weight, feinting for the head and switching to a ferocious hook to the body. The blow smashed into Anderson's gut as he raised both arms to shield his face, and the tall man grunted and doubled over to the impact. He tried to block the second punch on his arms, but it got through, slamming him hard on the jaw to knock his head back. Anderson reeled backwards from the onslaught, staggering to stand. Someone thrust out a boot behind him, clipping his heel, and he almost went down. Another blow crashed against his skull, and set his head ringing like a bull in a belltower, as Grierson came in again.

'Leave him be, Curt!' the prizefighter shouted. 'He's mine!'

Anderson lunged for the sound of the voice, swinging his clubbed fist with all his remaining strength. Shock tremored back through his arm as though he'd just hit rock, and Grierson swore through the blood in his mouth, coming ahead. The massive bulk of that black-shirted figure seemed to shut out the world, facing Anderson like an unscalable wall. He swung again, felt his arm go dead as a vicious counterpunch hammered his biceps. Grierson's next blow took him full in the throat, and for a while Anderson wondered if he'd quit breathing. He was still choking for air when a neatly aimed uppercut clipped the point of his chin, and put him down.

'Just you an' me this time, feller.' From above him, Grierson's mocking voice seemed a world away. 'Git up an' fight, you half-breed bastard!'

Venom of the insult got through to him, dragged him up from the dirt. Anderson made it to his feet, rocking unsteadily, eyes still struggling to focus as the big haymaker smashed into his face. This time he hardly felt it, going down like a log. Above him the voices blurred and faded to a jumble of sound that he couldn't make sense of. Besides, he was tired, and somebody was hauling a black sack over his head.

That was the last he remembered, before the sky fell on him.

CHAPTER FIVE

It was a hanging he was watching, some place he'd never been before. A fair-sized crowd was gathered by the foot of the gallows, although right now none of them could see him. Men swigging at bottles, while women

74

and youngsters waited eagerly for what was coming. Families out for a day's entertainment. It wasn't at them he looked, but at the lone figure standing on the gallows with both hands bound behind him, the noose of the hangrope already fitted about his neck. *Hombre* raised his head, and looked towards him, and he recognized the fierce, hawkish face of Diego Galvan.

He tried to call out, but the words froze like a sheath of ice on his lips, and no sound came. Hangman threw the lever, and the body crashed down through the trap, jerking violently before hanging like a weighted sack from the rope. Searing pain circled his throat, crushing the windpipe to choke the breath out of him. And as he died, he knew that his face was the face he had seen above the noose. The face of his friend, Diego Galvan.

'No!' Somehow he managed to shout through bursting lungs, though even as he did so he knew it was impossible, that he couldn't be dying. 'No! They won't hang Galvan!'

He shuddered, eyes opening suddenly to the darkness above him. Pain returned with consciousness, flowered like fire in his face and body. Anderson groaned, the memory coming back to him. His face was bruised and pounded like a raw side of beef, with a swelling forming under his right eye, and both lips were cut. He tried to stretch out, and fresh pain clawed him. From the feel of it, he'd got himself the mother

75

and father of a bruise in his mid-section, just above the belly. Grierson could punch the way a mule could kick, and that was the truth.

Questing search of his eyes found carved wooden beams of a ceiling above his head, made out the shape of walls and a window with the blinds drawn down. He was lying on a bed, naked but for his denim pants, his battered upper body swathed in bandages. From here, he couldn't see his boots, or the gunbelt they'd made him take off before he got his beating.

Only when movement stirred to his right, and he felt the gentle touch of a hand on his arm, did he realize that she was in the room with him.

'You are awake, Andres?' Josefa leaned over him, peering into his face. She held him back as he tried to rise from the bed. 'Lie still, Andres. Do not tax yourself further.'

'What happened? How'd you find me?' Sound of the words came strangely, forcing its way painfully through swollen lips. Above him, Josefa smiled sadly, lifting a hand to push back the errant lock of hair from her face.

'Raul followed you, with the dogs. They led him to you.' Abruptly her smile vanished, the handsome features sombre in reflection. 'It was lucky they found you so soon. My poor Andres, you have suffered much for us, I think.'

'Don't worry, I ain't lookin' for no fist-fight with Grierson again,' Anderson spoke through the pain of his bruises, angered a little by the pity in her voice. 'What about the three *pistoleros*, then? Did Raul see them?'

'*Verdad.*' Josefa nodded, her own strong features showing her revulsion at the thought. 'The others were Copeland's creatures also. He saw them ride away as he came to you, the noise of the dogs must have scared them.'

'Or they figured they didn't have time for a double murder,' Anderson decided. The dark man thought back to what had happened earlier, nodded at last. 'Could be it was lucky in more ways than one, Josefa. He didn't give them chance to look around.'

'Do not trouble over them.' Her voice pleaded with him, concern showing plain in the dark, deep-set eyes. 'You have already done much for us, Andres. Too much, perhaps.'

'That ain't how I see it, Josefa.' Anderson's look searched the dark corners of the room, hungrily. 'How long have I been here, anyhow?'

'Most of the day, since Raul brought you here. It is now evening.' Sensing his restless search of the room, Josefa sighed. 'No need to worry, Andres. Your guns are safe with us, your horse is being cared for by Martin in the stables. What is more important, you have no broken bones, and you will live. If they had killed you too, I would never have forgiven myself!'

Her voice shook over the last of the words,

and for a moment she turned away from him, her hand up to her face. Anderson reached over awkwardly, wincing as he clasped the other hand that still rested on his arm.

'Take it easy, huh?' The dark man forced a wry, bruised smile. 'I'm here, ain't I? That's somethin' I got to thank you an' Raul for, at least.' He paused, frowning as he thought about what he'd just said, and the other questions that still had to be answered. 'Josefa, I reckon I got somethin' to tell you. Somethin' important.'

He waited as she brushed once more at her face and turned to him again, her smooth Indian features calm and composed.

'What is it that you wish to say, Andres?' Josefa asked.

'Found somethin' in the woods by the line shack,' Anderson spoke softly, eyes wary on the shadows in the room. 'Espinoza wasn't murdered there, Josefa. They killed him in the woods, an' moved the body to the shack.'

'You know the ones who killed him?' All of a sudden Josefa's face seemed paler than before, her eyes wild and startled. Catching their expression, Anderson frowned for an instant, feeling her hand tighten beneath his own on the bed.

'Got me an idea, is all.' The dark man still frowned, his battered mouth forming the words with difficulty. 'Sure wasn't Diego, an' that's a fact. An' Copeland is behind it, I'm

78

willin' to bet. Some other things I ain't figured yet, mostly about the gun. Once we find the answers, ain't no way they kin hang Diego. You got my word on that, Josefa.'

'You have been a good friend to us both, Andres.' Josefa met his gaze uneasily, her face growing a sadder, rueful look. 'Maybe more than some of us deserve.'

She turned her head away for a moment, glancing back towards the dark outline of the doorway beyond. On the bed Anderson grimaced, fought up on to one elbow, biting his lip as the bruised pain moved with him.

'Andres, what are you doing?' Josefa turned back quickly towards him, but he warded her off. Anderson struggled to a sitting position on the edge of the bed, and began to look for his boots.

'Gonna need your help, Josefa.' The dark man gritted the words through his teeth, stooping to pick up his boots from the floor. 'You reckon you kin find someone to ride over to Teofilo Hernandez at Willow Creek? Tell him to expect some friends there before daylight?'

'If you wish it, Andres. Martin will go, or one of the *vaqueros*.' She watched him anxiously as he dragged on the boots, and pulled on the buckskin shirt painfully over his head. 'What is it you mean to do now? You are hurt, you must rest...'

'Been restin' here most of the day, Josefa.

Reckon that's long enough.' Anderson had found his hat, tugged it on over his lank black hair. Now he pushed to his feet, wincing as he crossed the room to where the gunbelt hung on a peg from the wall. 'Best you don't know where I'm headed, Josefa. Just do like I say, an' it ought to work.'

'Andres!' Her voice reached for him as he took down the belt, buckling it awkwardly about his waist. 'Andres, wait! There is something else that I must tell you...'

He heard the troubled, unsure sound of the words as they were framed, halted for a moment to look back. Anderson met Josefa's frightened gaze in the darkness of the room, and twisted his torn mouth to a reassuring smile.

'If it's what I think it is, Josefa, it'll keep,' he told her. He secured the belt in place, checking the holstered pistol for weight and balance before he returned it to leather. 'Once Martin gits back, stay here an' stick tight. I aim to settle this business one way or the other.'

'Take care, Andres.' Josefa, too, made a vain attempt to smile.

'Don't I always?' Anderson winced as pain stung in his bruised mouth. He turned, ducking out through the open doorway. 'Be seein' you, Josefa.'

She heard the muffled noise of his booted feet on the stairs below, and soon after it the closing of the outer door. Josefa didn't move to

80

the window to watch him go, turning back to the chair by the side of the empty bed. The tall *hacendada* sat down wearily, her hands clasped together. Stayed there, waiting for the night.

* * *

It was full dark by the time he reached Hillsburg, stars showing as bright, distant fires in the black depths of the sky above the town. He came in by the waste lots and corrals behind the row of buildings, the black horse picking its way through the busted cans and the mounds of rotting trash where the rats fought and scurried. Night wind gusted across the open ground and Anderson flinched as it caught the bruised flesh on his face, the pain of his hammered body knifing at him as he guided his mount in towards the rear of the jailhouse. Once there he dismounted, dropping the animal's rein over a leaning fence-post to anchor it for the present. The dark man cut through the nearest alleyway, ignoring the thin-ribbed dogs that skulked in the shadows to watch him pass. He made it to the corner of the block, and moved in on the tethered horses at the hitchrail out front. A big skewbald gelding took his eye, and he edged in beside it, talking to the nervous animal in a low-voiced Spanish he'd picked up from an old Mexican horse-breaker years before. Once he had it calmed, he loosed the rope from the crosspole and led it clear, heading back towards the alley.

The night wind blew a few stray tumbleweeds down Front Street, bowling them up against the walk, but apart from the weeds and the scavenging dogs no other life could be seen. From inside Walsh Hindman's saloon came raucous laughter, and the tinny notes of a piano jangling out what he figured had to be 'Streets of Laredo', though from the sound of it the feller who was playing wasn't any too sure himself. Somebody yelled out loudly, and he reckoned he heard the crash of a breaking chair. Things were livening up, all right. Anderson ducked back around the corner with the skewbald in tow as the first drunk of the night weaved out through the doors and sank heavily on to the boardwalk, spewing his liquor into the street.

He left the stolen horse fence-roped by the black, and went back along the alley he'd come down a moment before. Anderson stepped up on to the boardwalk and over to the door of the jailhouse. Knocked softly with his aching knuckles on the wood, and waited. After a while, the door eased part-way open.

'Anderson! What in hell . . .?' Mike Riordan stared at the dark man, taking in the mauled features and swollen eye in startled disbelief. Anderson raised a finger to his lips, and the gangling deputy nodded, lowering the carbine he held to pull back the door. He went back inside the room, setting the weapon down as

Anderson edged through and shut the door behind him.

'This is one heck of a time to come callin', ain't it?' Mike still hadn't got over his surprise, staring at the battered figure of the man in front of him. 'What happened to you, feller? Looks like ye've been hammered to hell an' back again.'

'Close enough, I reckon.' Anderson eased away from the door, grimacing as he flexed the bruised muscles of his belly. 'Ran into Grierson an' a couple of his pals on JD land, figured they weren't too pleased to see me.' He paused, glancing around the room which, but for the two of them, appeared to be empty. 'Where's Hatch?'

'Over at Juana's *cantina*, 'cross the street. It's where he eats most nights.' The lanky redhead shrugged, carried the carbine to the spur-scarred desk and laid it down. 'You wanted to talk to him, maybe?'

'No Mike.' Anderson forced his punished lips to a placating, apologetic smile. 'Reckon it's Diego I come to see. Got a message from Josefa he oughta hear, it's kind of important.'

'Uhuh.' Mike's long, good-natured features betrayed a hint of sympathy. 'Ain't been nothin' but trouble for her, I guess, an' none of it her doin'.' He left the carbine lying, moving across for the cell where Galvan had already risen to his feet and now stood eyeing Anderson uncertainly. 'You better come on

83

over an' tell him, *amigo*.'

'Figured you'd say that, Mike,' Anderson told him.

He drew the .45 Colt Army from its holster in one smooth, unhurried move, cocking and lining the weapon on the deputy's middle as Riordan froze in shock. The redhead stared at the gun uncomprehendingly, his desperate glance shifting to the carbine by the desk.

'Don't even think about it, Mike.' Anderson's voice came flat and hard, merciless as the black muzzle of the gun he held. 'I'm here to spring Diego out of that cell, an' that's what's gonna happen. Only way I use this pistol is if you make me. *Sabe usted?*'

'Don't worry, I ain't that dumb.' Riordan eyed the levelled Colt, forgetting about the carbine for the moment.

'So git the keys, an' turn him loose,' the dark man ordered.

Mike Riordan grabbed the bunch of keys from the desk, and went back to unlock the cell. He moved aside to let Galvan out through the barred door, looking to Anderson. 'How come you're doin' this?' The deputy's horsy face frowned in puzzled anger. 'No way you're gonna git away with it. Trial ain't due yet, anyhow.'

'Let's say I don't trust lynch mobs, OK?' Anderson motioned Galvan to stand clear of the door. 'Now give him the keys an' git inside.'

'You sure know how to take advantage of a

84

feller, don't you?' Riordan's tone was bitter. He handed over the keys, stepping into the cell, and the Mexican locked the door. Galvan came quickly towards the desk, his hawkish features breaking to a smile.

'You are here, as I hoped, *amigo*.' The big, grey-haired rancher eyed him gratefully, tossing the cell keys on the desk top. Galvan tugged open a drawer and dug hurriedly inside, pulled out his gun and gunbelt from its depths. '*Mil gracias*, Andres.'

'Save it for later, Diego.' Anderson headed for the back door of the jailhouse, his hard-eyed gaze moving back to where Mike Riordan glowered resentfully at him from behind the bars. 'No noise until we're gone, Mike. That way, none of us gits hurt, all right?'

'I hear you.' The deputy's voice was sullen. Riordan gripped the bars, anger plain in his kindly, unhandsome features. 'I'll be a while forgettin' this, Anderson, an' that's a promise!'

'*Adios*, Mike!' Anderson opened the door and dived out into the night, the gaunt figure of the rancher plunging after him. Galvan was still buckling on the gunbelt as they stumbled through the trash and busted cans in the dark, making for the spot where the two horses snorted and tugged on their ropes. Behind them in the cell they could hear the angry yelling of the imprisoned deputy.

'Hey, Hatch! Git over here! They just sprung Galvan!'

Anderson reached the sagging fence post, flipped the halters loose. He hauled himself into the saddle and gathered the rein, holding on to the skewbald's rope as the scared animal tried to back away, tugging against him.

'Git aboard, *amigo!*' Anderson shouted. Abruptly he lowered his voice, trying to calm the frightened beast. 'Easy there, boy. Easy now.'

Skewbald stopped fighting the rope for an instant, and the Mexican got himself into the saddle. Galvan seized the rein from Anderson, held tight as the big horse plunged and threw up its head. He turned the animal with an effort, touched heels to its flanks as Anderson and his mount set off at a run through the waste lots behind the street. The skewbald blew down its nostrils and darted forward, breaking to a headlong gallop across the littered ground. By the time the first townsfolk heard Riordan's cries and came out on to the walk, the two horsemen were clear of Hillsburg, and deep into the brush.

'Seems to me horse-stealin' is gittin' a way too easy, these days,' Anderson said. He held rein as the black struck a measured lope beneath him, Galvan and the skewbald keeping pace as they broke through the last of the thickets. 'Wasn't a soul out there to see me lift that critter tonight. Hatch is growin' slack in his old age, I reckon.'

He grinned wryly at the thought, winced as

86

pain reminded him of the punishment he'd taken. Alongside him Diego Galvan grinned less surely in answer, his dark gaze questioning on the figure of his rescuer.

'So now we are horse-thieves also.' The Mexican shrugged expressively, his gaunt face almost youthful in the cold starlight. '*No importa*, they cannot hang me more than once. What is your plan, *amigo*?'

'We go to Teofilo, at Willow Creek,' Anderson told him. 'I already sent word for him to expect us. Reckon he'll hide us for a while.'

'They will follow our tracks, from Hillsburg,' Galvan reminded him, and the dark man nodded.

'Yeah.' Anderson's painful smile was slyer than before. 'I thought of that, too.' He said nothing more, and the pair of them stayed quiet for a spell, only the thud of hooves in the dirt and the rattle of thorns on leather breaking the night-time stillness. Somewhere out of sight an owl hooted, and Anderson figured he heard the faint, shrill scream of a vole as the bird swooped on its prey. Beyond the brush came wooded country, pine and juniper furring the slopes that led south for Willow Creek.

'You are hurt, Andres. Who did this to you?' Galvan's voice broke in on him suddenly, echoing against the quiet. Turning, Anderson saw the fierce hawkish face drawn tight with

87

anger, the eyes black, glinting stones in the flesh. 'Tell me who is responsible, my friend, and I will make them answer for it!'

'Nothin' to worry about, Diego. Three of Copeland's bunch, is all.' Anderson gritted his teeth as the movement of the stallion jolted his bruised body, losing the smile. 'Tell truth, I reckon it was worth it. Right now we got enough proof to clear you of the murder, *amigo*. Copeland is back of it, just like I thought.'

'He is a *serpiente*, a reptile.' Galvan puckered and spat from the saddle, his gaunt face showing its disgust. Then the weight of the other's words hit through to him, and he stared, as if not fully believing what he heard. 'You have proof? Does this mean you know who the murderer is, the one who killed Espinoza?'

'Maybe.' Anderson eyed the country ahead, sober-faced as the horse took him towards the first of the timber. 'Some loose ends to clear up, I reckon.'

'If this is so, why did you rescue me?' the Mexican wanted to know.

'Friend Copeland has plenty of tricks,' Anderson told him. 'Wouldn't put it past him to fix up a lynch mob an' break into the jailhouse, if he figured I was on to him. That way he wouldn't need a trial at all.' Meeting the other man's gaze, he found time for the faintest of smiles. 'Havin' you loose upsets his plans,

Diego. He's gonna have to come out in the open an' make his play. That's when we put paid to him, I reckon.'

'Let us hope so, Andres.' Galvan didn't sound quite so sure. The gaunt Mexican stole a glance to the man beside him. 'What of Josefa, my friend? She is well?'

'Well as can be. She sends her best.' Anderson frowned thoughtfully as the stallion slowed to a walk, moving cautiously in among the trees. 'She knows about this, Diego, but I figured it's best she stays clear until we run Copeland down. That's one hell of a woman you got there, feller. Better believe it.'

'I know it.' Galvan's features, too, showed grave and troubled. 'All the same, you do well to remind me, my friend. This last year, with the work of the ranch, and other things, perhaps I have not always been as a husband should. *Entiende?*'

Riding alongside, Anderson nodded, saying nothing.

'You know, Andres, that I would not tell this to any other man?'

'Sure, Diego.' Anderson didn't look towards him, still guiding his mount through the trees. 'Ain't nobody else gonna hear it, neither. You got my word on that.'

'I am grateful to you, Andres.' The sound of the Mexican's voice turned his head, brought him face to face with the dark, intent scrutiny of those eyes. Galvan searched the face of his

89

rescuer, as if anxious to be understood. 'Before, you have saved my life. Now you come many miles to help us again. It is a debt I cannot pay, *amigo*.'

'No reason why you should,' Anderson grinned, for the moment disregarding the pain from his battered features. 'We're friends, Diego. What else did you expect me to do, once I got word?'

'I will not forget this, my friend,' Galvan told him, and the dark man nodded.

'Reckon that's all the payment I need,' Anderson said.

He took the stallion forward, man and horse following the uphill slope through the trees.

Night was halfway through when they came out from the timber, and down the last slopes to Willow Creek. The *adobe casa* showed up in the midst of the grassland with its scatter of *piñon* and juniper trees, the outbuildings huddling close against it, a frame *ramada*, and a couple of lean-to *jacals* with their makeshift roofs of sod and brush. The outline of the house shone pale against the darkness, and the riders made towards it. Some distance from the *casa* they heard the noise of barking, and a pair of big, brindled sheepdogs came bouncing across the shadowed grass to meet them.

'*Hola*, Coronel! Capitan!' It was a young man who called out to them, whistling to halt the dogs in their tracks. He came out from the house, white of his cotton shirt and pants

90

etched sharply against the night, and stood to face the horsemen as they reined in short of the sheepdogs, now lying prone in readiness for further orders.

'*Buenos noches*, Marcelo,' Anderson said.

'*Buenos noches*, Señor Anderson.' Marcelo Hernandez had been no more than a kid when Anderson came here last. Over the past six years he'd grown to manhood, his muscled body lithe and slender, the boyish face showing its first growth of beard. 'You are welcome here. You also, Señor Galvan.'

'*Gracias*.' The rancher eyed the youthful, stalwart figure, evidently impressed. 'And your father, Señor Hernandez. He is here?'

'I am here, Señor Galvan.' Teofilo had followed his son from the house with the rest of the family, who now stood in a group behind the younger man. The small, thin-featured *pastor* smiled, eyes bright and alert in the weatherbeaten face. 'We are not accustomed to cattlemen as guests, but for friends of Señor Anderson we are prepared to make exceptions. Dismount, and come with us. *Esta su casa*.'

'For a herdsman, you are not so bad, Hernandez,' Galvan smiled in answer, doffing his *sombrero* to the plump figure of the woman by Teofilo's side. '*Buenos noches, senora*.'

'*Buenos noches*, Señor Galvan.' Abrana Hernandez, like her husband, was a little greyer than when Anderson had seen her last, her round face growing a few more wrinkles in places. All the same, when she smiled Anderson's way he figured she was still a real pleasure to the eye. 'It is good to see you once more, Señor Anderson. This meeting has been too long in coming.'

'For me too, Abrana,' the dark man told her.

'Martin Quiroga came from the ranch with a message,' Teofilo broke in on them, his dark eyes questioning the two horsemen. 'He says you need our help. What can we do for you, Andres, my good friend?'

'They want to hang Diego for a murder he did not commit,' Anderson told the little herder. He scanned the huddle of buildings as he spoke, as if searching for a likely hiding-place. 'I have proof that others killed Manuel Espinoza, but I cannot tell the sheriff until I am certain. Until then, I trust you to hide my friend Diego Galvan, and see that no harm comes to him.'

'We shall do this, Andres,' Teofilo answered gravely, his glance going northward to the timbered slopes beyond. 'They will be following you from Hillsburg, *verdad*?'

'*Verdad.*' Anderson took the halter-rope of the skewbald from Galvan's hand, motioning to him to dismount. 'They will come here, perhaps in two hours. I shall lead them away from here, if you help me.'

'In what way, my friend?'

'You have made sacking shoes before, Teofilo?' Anderson was smiling. Catching the sly glint in his eye, the *pastor* also smiled.

'It shall be done at once, Andres!' Hernandez turned, heading back for the house. The *pastor* called out to the others as he went. 'Abrana! Marcelo! Come with me. Ruben, take our guest to the barn, and hide him there!'

'*Seguro*, Señor Hernandez.' The old, white-haired Mexican herder at the rear of the group spoke for the first time, moving forward. Ruben Garcia couldn't be far short of eighty now, Anderson figured, but although the stooping shoulders betrayed his age, the jet-black stare was keen and penetrating. Seeing Anderson, the oldster smiled and ducked his head in greeting. '*Buenos noches*, Señor Anderson. You are welcome here, even under such circumstances, be sure.'

'I know it, Ruben.' Anderson watched as Galvan got down from his mount, and he and the old herder exchanged their greetings. 'I should be back in a while, Diego. Meantime, you best do like Ruben tells you.'

'*Gracias*, Andres, and good luck,' the grey-haired rancher told him.

'If you will come with me now, Señor Galvan.' Ruben doffed his straw *sombrero*, pointing with it towards the barn. Galvan smiled in answer, his teeth showing white through the thick moustache.

'*Con mucho gusto*, Señor Garcia.'

He followed the older man towards the barn, the dogs moving back for the house. Anderson

93

sat his horse, holding the skewbald by its rope, and waited. It wasn't any too long before Teofilo and the others returned, hurrying to rejoin him.

'Your shoes, Andres.' Abrana handed them to him, her plump face beaming with pride.

'They are magnificent, Abrana,' Anderson told her. He stowed the small pockets of sacking with their rawhide ties into the saddle-bags, nodding his thanks. 'They will serve well for what I have in mind.'

He turned the black with a touch of the rein, and started away from the house, the led skewbald following. Maybe twenty yards further on he glanced back to the small group who stood by the *casa*, watching him go.

'I will be back before the posse comes,' Anderson said. He smiled reassuringly. 'The sheriff is a good man, he will not harm you. If you tell him we forced you to help us, and rode on into the woods, he will believe you, I think.'

'*Vaya con Dios*, Andres,' Teofilo said.

The dark man ducked his head in acknowledgement, nudging the black horse forward. Anderson rode out around the huddle of buildings, and off towards Willow Creek.

Maybe now they had a chance, he thought.

CHAPTER SIX

The line of the creek cut across the open grassland before him, a bright snaking gleam through its veil of cottonwoods and willows. Above, the stars had begun to fade, sky paling from inky black to a dull bluish grey as the night retreated. Anderson rode his mount down into the creek, leading the second horse after him. He took both animals a half-mile or so downstream before turning off to the left, making a wide loop through the grassland and coming in from another angle to climb the slope that led back into the timber.

Once into the trees he went steadily, guiding the black and the skewbald through the stands of oak and ponderosa pine. Anderson scoured the shadowed stretches between the trees, on the alert for any more surprises. The dark man frowned as he rode, his hard-planed Indian features grim as stone. He was thinking about that stolen pistol, and how it had come into the hands of the murderers. By now, he reckoned he'd ruled out Martin Quiroga. The youngster may have disliked Espinoza, but he didn't have the cunning needed for a trick of that kind, and he was loyal to Josefa. Raul had the wit, all right, and maybe the motive, but unless he was playing some devious kind of double game he would have had no reason to rescue Anderson from Grierson and his bunch. And if he hated Espinoza, he wouldn't have relied on Copeland, whom he hated even more. Anderson shook his head, frowning still as he topped a rise and went downhill through the trees. Trouble was, if he ruled out Martin and Raul, that only left one other as far as he could see. And why would Manuel Espinoza have stolen a gun that was going to kill him?

Second question had to be, what exactly was Copeland after? Sure, he wanted the ranch, and probably Teofilo's land with its water rights, but cattle ranches weren't too uncommon in this part of New Mexico. Certainly not unusual enough to attract a Chicago syndicate, anyhow. If Hatch had been telling him straight, Copeland was some kind of front man for the organization back East, and that had to mean something big. Anything sizeable enough to hire Lon Mather just in case was way out of any cattle rancher's league. Anderson swore, struck away to the right where another bend of the creek flowed into the timber. Damned if he knew what it was they had in mind, but it was something more than grassland and cattle herds.

There was more to Ross Copeland than met the eye. More to Espinoza, too, he figured. Until he discovered all there was to know about them, and until he had all the answers, there was no way he could make the whole thing fit.

The dark man breathed out sharply in annoyance, dismissing the thoughts from his mind. Right now he had one job to perform, and that was to lead Hatch's posse on a wild-goose chase. Once they were shaken off, maybe he and Galvan could do a little more investigating. And if they were lucky, this latest move might throw Copeland into giving something else away.

He ran both horses into the bend of the creek and turned back southward, moving upstream against the current. After wading in the water for a few minutes he turned off right, leaving the creek to strike uphill through a thick stand of brush that promised to hide most of the tracks. Anderson made it through the thicket and into a ponderosa clump, shielded by brush and willows from anyone fording the creek below, and screened from above by more stands of timber. Here he dismounted and tethered the horses while he unshipped the sacking overshoes. The set he always carried fitted the black without any trouble, and the ones he'd taken from Abrana went onto the big skewbald's hooves with room to spare, though he had more trouble putting them on. The animal was unused to them, and shied once in a while, but Anderson had foreseen the problem, and soothed the critter down. Once they were reshod and the rawhide ties drawn together, he took off his boots and donned the old moccasins he'd used since the Victorio war, back in '81. Anderson ran a rawhide thong through the mule-ears and hung the boots around his neck. He untethered the horses and mounted up, heading back towards the Hernandez place.

He took the horses another mile or so deeper into the timber, until he found a spot where the trees stood thick and close together, tangled with brushy undergrowth. Anderson dismounted and led the black and the skewbald into the clump of trees, and tethered them. He fed both animals a little grain from his saddle-bags before he left, unshipping the saddles from their backs. Anderson unsheathed the Winchester .45-70 carbine from its scabbard, and moved out from the timber stand. At the edge of the trees he turned, looking back to the tethered horses.

'Take it easy, boys,' he murmured. 'I aim to be back before too long.'

He set off through the timber, heading up the slope.

Night was just about played out by now, the sky lightening to pearly grey above the trees. Anderson kept going, skirting around the timbered slopes to come in on the *casa* and its outbuildings from the far side. He made good time, moving lithely on moccasined feet over the tree litter and pine needles in the shadow of the ponderosa stands. The worst of the bruising was beginning to wear off, subsiding to a dull, nagging pain that reminded him of toothache. Boots around his neck hampered him a little, but not too much. At the side of the big, double-rigged Texas saddle he'd left behind, their weight didn't trouble him unduly. What occupied his mind most at present was the thought of that posse, and getting back to Teofilo's before they arrived.

He was almost clear of the timber, starting downhill to where the grassland and its scattered trees offered shelter, when his keen ears caught the faint clipping sound that came again. Faint, solid clip that a hoof might make, striking on a stone or twig. A moment later he heard the noise of a horse blowing uneasily down its nostrils as the animal scented him.

'Come out of there, feller!' Anderson called. He steadied the Winchester against his shoulder, sighting in the direction of the last sound he'd heard. 'I ain't here to fool around!'

'*No tiran*, Andres,' Josefa Galvan said.

She rode out cautiously from the shelter of the trees, keeping the roan mare to an easy walk. The black velvet riding-habit fitted her closely, set off her woman's figure with its smooth dark sheen, the divided skirt enabling her to ride astride in comfort. Anderson lowered the carbine, his glance taking in the white blouse and crimson bandanna, the black flat-topped hat whose wide brim shaded her face.

'Thought I told you to stay put, Josefa,' the dark man said.

'I am a *hacendada*, Andres. I am not good at taking orders,' She tried for a smile, and didn't quite make it. Josefa met the look of the dismounted rifleman, her dark eyes sad and troubled. 'Besides, Diego is my husband. How could I sit at the ranch, knowing him to be in danger of his life? It was not possible...'

'An' that's why you came out here, huh?' Anderson's gaze still questioned. Under its piercing scrutiny Josefa frowned and looked down, her handsome features uneasy.

'It was not my only reason.' She raised her head with what appeared to be an effort, forcing herself to look him in the eye. 'You will remember, Andres, that before you left, there was something I wished you to know...'

'It's you an' Espinoza, ain't it?' the dark man asked, and Josefa nodded.

'*Verdad*, Andres.' For a moment the tall woman closed her eyes, her hands clasped tight on the saddlehorn. When she opened them again, they rested fully on him. 'I think, from what you say, that you have already guessed, but you are risking your life for us here. It is best that you know the truth.'

She halted, eyes searching his face for any change of expression. Anderson's dark Indian features gave no hint of what he thought.

'Go ahead, Josefa. I'm listenin',' Anderson said.

'When he first came to work for us, we were glad,' Josefa told him. 'After Arcadio's death, many were afraid, and it seemed to us that Espinoza had courage to take on the job of *segundo*. He was a good cattleman, and his help was welcome. You understand, Andres?'

The dark man nodded, saying nothing.

'What I told you before, much of it was the truth.' The *hacendada* struggled a little over her words, bit on her lip for an instant. 'Before Copeland came here, Diego and I were happy. But since that time, we had grown more distant. The ranch, and the troubles that Copeland brought, took up much of his time, so that I did not see him so often. Also we wished for a child, and none came.'

She broke off, trying vainly to hold back the tears that welled suddenly in her eyes.

'You don't have to tell me any more, Josefa,' Anderson offered. At once she shook her head fiercely, choking to speak.

'You must hear it all, Andres!' Her voice struck at him, commanding him to silence. 'With Copeland's enmity towards us, matters became much worse. Diego began once more to drink on occasion, and there were quarrels. He was rarely in the house, but Manuel Espinoza was always there, for instructions or to ask advice. He was young, and tall, and handsome, a *vero hombre* who had shown his courage, or so I thought. When he began to show me attentions, a woman older than himself, I was flattered. I was a fool, Andres!'

'So he made love to you, while Diego was

away?' Anderson's voice held a weary, resigned sadness.

'As you say, Andres. Many times,' Josefa swallowed hard, her smooth face colouring at the memory. '*Quien sabe?* Perhaps it was not love, but some other thing that has no name. Often it was only the pleasure of our bodies, like the animals. But at other times, there was more, I think. My feelings for him were strong, and I was foolish enough to believe that he cared also.'

'So the bit about the gun, an' warnin' him off, that ain't the truth?'

'That was later, when I knew he meant to harm Diego.' The tall woman sighed, seeming not to notice the tears that ran unchecked down her face. 'He spoke of Diego disappearing and not returning, of the two of us owning the ranch together. It was then I saw that he loved only himself, and wished to take the ranch from us. Now I am ashamed of my foolishness, and there may be a child!'

She broke off again, sobbing openly. Anderson thought about that for a while, stroking a hand at the nape of his neck as his lean face sobered.

'Listen to me, Josefa,' he said. 'Six years back, you saved my life in a saloon gunfight back in Hillsburg, an' I ain't liable to forget it. As for what you just told me, maybe I ain't been spotless in that department neither, an' I sure as hell ain't no judge nor no reverend.

102

Espinoza you told me about. How 'bout Diego? You still want him back?'

'If he will have me.' Josefa choked on the words, brushing angrily at her smeared face.

'Good enough,' Anderson told her. 'You an' Diego are friends of mine, an' that's how it stays, you hear? Tell you somethin' else, Josefa. He'll take you back all right, an' I reckon he'd be a damn fool if he didn't.'

'You are too kind, Andres,' she began, and the dark man shook his head.

'Like hell I am, Josefa...' Same instant he framed the words, his ears caught on to another, more menacing sound. Dull drumming of many hooves, coming in towards them from a distance. Anderson grabbed the roan mare's halter and ran back for the cover of the trees, leading horse and rider after him.

'Get down, Josefa,' he murmured.

He gave back to the shadow of the trees as she hurried to dismount, and laid his hand over the muzzle of the roan. Anderson frowned, hearing the beat of the hooves come closer. Looked like they'd made better time than he expected.

Josefa was into cover behind him, her body pressed tight to the bole of a pine. The dark man forgot her for the moment, hefting the carbine one-handed as he kept the mare's mouth covered against any tell-tale sound. It hadn't been any plan of his to trade shots with Hatch and his posse, and he figured it wasn't

103

about to do him any good.

The thunder of the shod hooves grew louder, swelled to a roar that shook the ground. He saw the riders break momentarily into view between the trees, surging over the crest far to the right of Josefa and himself to plunge downhill for the *casa*. Tracks he'd left with Diego had been enough to draw them there, which was no surprise. What made him less comfortable was the figures of some of the distant riders. Hatch and Riordan headed the column of horsemen, and there appeared to be a fair scattering of townsfolk behind them, but even this far off the keen vision that had served him as an Army scout years before picked out other, less welcome shapes. Anderson caught sight of the black-shirted bulk of Hal Grierson, the spectrally tall silhouette of the gunhawk Lon Mather. Most startling of all was the thin, undersized figure in the Prince Albert and the derby hat, who rode close behind the lawmen. Seemed Ross Copeland was putting in an appearance, and he'd brought his friends along. Galvan's escape had spooked the son of a bitch, all right. Now it looked like he was out to make sure it didn't happen again. Watching as the riders poured over the crest and down from sight, the noise of the horses' hoofbeats fading slowly, the dark man ran his tongue around the inside of a mouth gone suddenly dry as a hide. He got the feeling that if it was Copeland's bunch who saw Diego first, the

Mexican wouldn't live to hang.

'You better git from here, Josefa,' he told the woman behind him. Anderson freed the roan's muzzle as silence returned, handed the rein back to the animal's owner. 'Ain't nothin' you kin do right now, I reckon.'

'What would you have me do, Andres?' Josefa set a foot to the stirrup, swinging up across the horse's back as she asked the question. Eyeing her for a moment, the dark man sighed, hefting the carbine on to his shoulder.

'Go back to the ranch,' he told her. 'Have your *vaqueros* armed and ready to ride, just in case. I aim to lie low until dark, down at the *casa*. If I ain't showed up by this time tomorrow, come lookin'. OK?'

'I will do this, be sure.' Josefa's smudged face had regained its determination. The tall woman nodded grimly, reached from the saddle to grasp his hand for an instant. 'My thanks to you, Andres. *Muchas gracias.*'

'*Por nada.*' Anderson stood back as she released her hold, shifted the weight of the boots that hung from his neck. 'Just git out of here fast, all right?'

'*Vaya con Dios*, Andres.'

'*Vaya con Dios*, Josefa.'

He watched as she turned the big mare around, heading back at a gallop through the timber stands. Anderson didn't wait to see her disappear into the pines, already running for

105

the wooded patches lower down the slope. He moved quickly, covering the open stretches between the trees with the stealthy swiftness he had inherited from his mother's people, flitting almost without sound from one clump of timber to the next. When the trees gave out and cover no longer reached head-high he went lower, working his way through the tall grama grass on elbows and knees, keeping the carbine out in front of him as he moved. Slower and more strenuous than upright movement, the crawling cost him time, and he hauled into cover behind a thick tussock that overlooked the last of the slope, peering down. The horsemen were already there, just like he'd figured. And from this close, he could hear their voices.

'Come on outa there, Hernandez!' Hatch bellowed. 'We want to talk to you, feller!'

The little sheriff hauled on the rein as he shouted, pulling his mount to a halt in the open ground fronting the house. Beside him lanky Mike Riordan got quickly down from the saddle, gun drawn as he lined on the *casa* doorway. Watching, Anderson guessed that the deputy wasn't in the best of tempers after last night, and felt a twinge of conscience. None of this business was Mike's fault, after all. He wished the same could be said of Ross Copeland and his gunhands, who now also hurried to dismount, closing in on the house.

'You heard him, you greaser bastard!' That

106

was Grierson, his ugly voice thick with menace. The black-clad *hombre* levelled his gun on the door as he spoke. 'Come on out, or you gonna be sorry!'

Tall, blond Lon Mather said nothing, his own pistol balanced idly in his palm as he watched the house. Among the men around him Anderson picked out big Walsh Hindman in his hickory shirt, and the shorter gunman they called Nathan Coe. Fisher stood further back with Copeland, close to the horses, looking on and smiling. Anderson tightened his grip on the carbine, his bruised mouth clenched. So far, he hadn't done too well against this bunch, he figured, but he aimed to alter that, and soon.

'*Señores!*' The voice of Teofilo Hernandez called from inside the house. 'No need for shooting, *señores*! We are coming out, and none of us have guns!'

He opened the door and stepped outside with both hands raised, the others following close behind. Ruben and Abrana had their hands lifted to show they held no weapons, while Marcelo gripped the snarling sheepdogs by their collars. At sight of the small, unarmed group, most of the possemen lowered their guns. Only Copeland's gunhawks kept their weapons levelled, their faces revealing a thwarted anger.

'So where's Anderson, Mex?' Lon Mather asked.

107

He spoke softly, so that Anderson had to strain to catch the words, but there was no mistaking the chill threat in his tone. Teofilo eyed the pistol and the tall man behind it, licked nervously at his lips before he answered.

'They were here, *señor*,' the little herder admitted. 'Two hours, perhaps. *Quien sabe?* Maybe more than that. They forced us to feed them, and water their horses, then rode away north into the timber.' Looking to the furious face of the sheriff, he spread his hands helplessly. '*Señores*, they had guns. What could we do?'

'You better be tellin' the truth, Hernandez,' Hatch scowled, his hard blue eyes raking the outbuildings and the land around. 'Mike, go search the house. You other fellers take a look at the barn an' the shacks.'

'Sure thing, Tate.' Mike Riordan ran towards the house, and plunged inside. Wasn't more than a few minutes before he reappeared, frowning and shaking his head. By then, most of the posse were headed for the outbuildings.

'Check the tracks, Curt,' Ross Copeland spoke quietly to the thin, sandy-haired gunman beside him. Fisher set off at a run round the farside of the house, big Walsh Hindman hurrying to follow him.

'These people have helped Anderson before, Sheriff.' It was Copeland who spoke again, his voice carrying to where Hatch sat his horse in front of the house. His cold stare rested on

Teofilo Hernandez in the same moment. 'It's my opinion they are none of them to be trusted.'

'Maybe so, Mister Copeland.' Hatch tried vainly to hide the impatience in his voice. The sheriff patted the neck of his fretting mount, watching as his men scoured the outbuildings. 'Right now we got 'em here unarmed, an' they ain't givin' us no trouble. Unless we find out different, ain't no way I kin prove they're lyin'.'

'What's wrong with you, Hatch?' Grierson broke in again, the sneer distorting his unlovely features. 'You gittin' a taste for greasers in your old age, maybe?'

'That's enough, Hal!' Copeland's whiplash voice struck the thickset man to silence before the furious lawman could answer. The rancher met Hatch's angry stare, his own cold green eyes unrelenting. 'There's truth in what he says, Sheriff. Anderson is a horsethief and the accomplice of a murderer. If you go soft on these people now, it could reflect badly on you later.'

'Like at the election for county sheriff, for instance?' Hatch had taken enough, and it showed. The stocky figure of the sheriff tensed in the saddle, his round face a beetroot shade as he yelled at the man in the derby. 'Maybe you're right, Mister Copeland, but as long as I'm sheriff what I say goes, an' don't you forget it. Ain't no way I need no jumped-up rancher to tell me my job, you hear?'

'You got no right to talk to Mister Copeland that way!' Grierson shouted. The burly man rounded on the sheriff, bringing up his unsheathed pistol. Lon Mather took a firm grip on the prizefighter's arm, forcing it downward. Grierson took one look at the hard, weathered features of the taller gunman, and was quiet.

'Your attitude in this case is to be regretted, Sheriff.' Copeland had regained his icy calm. All the same his yellow-fleshed face showed tight and pale, his eyes glinting like shards of emerald glass. 'No doubt in the near future we shall see who regrets it the most.'

Hatch didn't answer, glaring furiously at the rancher. Around the house the rest of the possemen trooped back dejectedly from their search of the outbuildings, and Fisher and Hindman came back at a run looking a whole lot happier.

'Tracks out the back, boss!' Fisher grinned, his voice sharp and eager. 'Two horses, an' headed north, just like he said!'

He spoke to Copeland, ignoring the angry figure of Hatch closer to him. The thin-faced rancher frowned thoughtfully as the words were spoken, glanced questioningly to the bigger, heavyset figure of Walsh Hindman.

'It's them, Mister Copeland.' The saloonman nodded, scratching nervously at his black-stubbled jaw. 'Same horses we been trailin' here, cuttin' back into the timber. We

110

follow 'em now, oughta nail 'em for sure.'

Copeland said nothing, a thin smile forming on his narrow, yellow-fleshed face.

'OK, that's all!' Hatch yelled at the returning possemen, already setting his horse forward. 'Ain't nothin' here, I reckon. Let's git after them, *pronto*!' He reined in for a moment as the others ran hunting their saddles, his glance cutting back to the group of Mexicans in the *casa* doorway. 'This better be right, Hernandez! Anderson has plenty to answer for, right now. You help him, you're in big trouble!'

'*Señor*,' Teofilo bowed his dark, greying head. The grave features of the *pastor* betraying nothing of what he thought.

Hatch swore, and touched heels to the sides of his mount, the horse carrying him around the far side of the house. Copeland and his bunch were among the first to follow, a cursing Mike Riordan not far behind. The posse struck away from the house, and out across the grassland, hitting to a gallop as they picked up the tracks again.

Anderson stayed watching until they were almost out of sight before working his way forward on elbows and knees as before. Not until he was within a few yards of the house itself did he risk standing upright, and walking the distance that remained. Teofilo and the others were still in the doorway, waiting to meet him.

'It has worked, Andres?' the herder asked, and the dark man nodded.

'For now, anyhow.' Anderson conjured up a grin of relief. '*Mil gracias, amigo.*'

'*Por nada.*' Teofilo took him by the arm, leading him towards the barn. 'Come with me, my friend. It is your turn to hide, I think.'

Once inside the big frame *ramada* Teofilo led him to the far corner of the building, shoving away the bales of straw to reveal a trapdoor in the floor beneath. The *pastor* used a heavy iron ring in the door to lift it, and ushered Anderson down stone steps to the cool darkness of a cellar where provisions were stored. There Diego Galvan crouched in the gloom, squatting with both hands resting on his knees. Seeing Anderson, the grey-haired Mexican grinned broadly, getting to his feet.

'We have fooled them, *amigo?*' Galvan queried, and Anderson shrugged, setting down his carbine by the wall.

'Looks like it.' The dark man settled himself beside the weapon, thumbing back the hat on his head. Anderson unshipped the boots, and laid them on the ground. 'Right now we got Copeland runnin' scared, an' that has to be good.'

'*Muy bien.*' The hawkish face showed its approval, the deep-set eyes gleaming against the darkness. 'What is your next move, my friend?'

'Come nightfall, I'll go back an' collect the

horses,' Anderson told him. 'Could be I'll pay a call on Mister Copeland before too long. He hadn't figured on you bein' sprung, Diego, an' he might just make a mistake or two.'

'I will leave you now, my friends,' Teofilo smiled, starting back up the steps. 'In a little while, Ruben will bring you food and drink. When it is first dark, I will come for you.'

'*Gracias, amigo,*' Anderson said.

He and Diego watched as the herder went up out of sight, and the door clanged down to leave them in darkness. For a while neither of them spoke.

'You will take me with you, when you go?' the rancher asked at last.

'Reckon not,' Anderson spoke softly, frowning into the dark. 'Less they see of you, the better—for now, at least. Once I've checked out Copeland, we kin maybe take what we've got to Hatch, an' let him do it by the book. From what I seen, he's mad enough to go up agin Copeland right now.'

'That is a pity,' Galvan answered as quietly, his voice betraying no apparent emotion. 'I would have enjoyed speaking to Mister Copeland with you, I think.'

'In a while maybe, Diego.' Anderson still frowned, his mind seemingly someplace else. 'Tell me about Raul Nunez, *amigo.*'

'Raul Nunez?' Anderson sensed the puzzlement in the other's voice as Galvan turned to him in the gloom. 'What is there to

113

tell? He was once a *vaquero*, before a steer trampled him and damaged his shoulder. He has been with us almost five years as a steward to the house, his accounting is good. What else do you wish to know?'

'Not a thing.' Anderson settled his back against the wall, nodding thoughtfully. 'Just figured I'd ask, is all.'

He tipped the old Army hat forward over his face, and closed his eyes, waiting for nightfall.

CHAPTER SEVEN

He made it to cover in the trees. Halted there to regain his breath, his back braced against a pine trunk as he listened to the night. No sound answered from the heavy darkness around him, high boughs keeping off the light of moon and stars to shroud the timber in deep shadow. Anderson waited a while and nodded, satisfied. He moved quickly forward to the next patch of shelter that offered itself, breaking to a lunging run between the pines. He'd been here before, and knew his way even in the dark. And this time he didn't have his boots to carry.

Soft earth and mould gave underfoot, creaking faintly to the tread of his moccasins. Anderson didn't bother to look back down the slope to where Teofilo's *casa* made a pale blur against the surrounding gloom, hefting the

114

Winchester carbine as he loped ahead. He'd brought the weapon along just in case. Chances were that Hatch and the posse had turned back by now, but Copeland's gunhawks were a different matter. If there were any still lurking in the timber, he wasn't aiming to be outgunned.

Diego he'd left behind, once Teofilo let them out at nightfall. The big Mexican had seen him off with some reluctance, but Anderson figured he could depend on Galvan not to come running after. Not so long ago, Diego had been a gunfighter in this neck of the woods. He knew it didn't pay to take too many risks. Darting over the crest, deeper into the pines, Anderson frowned. Diego was no problem for the moment. He was the one out here risking himself, and right now he had other things to trouble his mind.

It had to be Manuel Espinoza who had stolen that pistol, he told himself. He'd figured it might be Raul Nunez for a while, but there wasn't any way the oldster would have done a deal with Copeland. Raul hadn't trusted Anderson when he found him nosing around the line shack, but he'd horned in to save him from Hal Grierson and his friends. Not out of any love for Anderson, maybe, but loyalty to his brand. Way he saw it, Raul wasn't the kind to doublecross the folks who paid his wages, and had given him a home when his career as a *vaquero* was finished. He wouldn't have set up

115

Galvan, nor would Martin. And that left only the *segundo*, the man who'd come to them looking for a job soon after the murder of Arcadio Gomez.

Heading through the last few stands of timber that separated him from the tethered horses, Anderson gripped the carbine, feeling the conviction grow more firmly in his mind. Espinoza hadn't shown up by accident, and he had some kind of connection with Copeland. Josefa had already told Anderson of the foreman's plans for Galvan's disappearance, and from the sound of things he'd been keen to get Diego out of the way. But why in heaven's name steal a gun that would later be used to shoot him dead?

One reason: Espinoza had no idea he was about to be murdered. Copeland, or whoever he'd used to spin the line, had fooled the *segundo* just as he'd fooled Josefa. Some other phoney excuse had been fed to him, some way of using the gun to discredit Diego Galvan. Maybe Espinoza had grown troublesome to his employers, threatened to spoil the plans they had made. Or maybe that had been the plan all along?

This minute, it was mostly guesswork, but Anderson sensed that he was headed in the right direction. So far, the guesses appeared to ring true, and if he put them together the whole thing began to fit, in a way it hadn't done before.

He was into the last of the ponderosa stands, making for the spot where he'd left the horses tethered, when the first sound warned him. Dry, popping noise of a twig that snapped under a booted foot, the echoes sounding after in the silence that followed. Anderson went low to the ground, crouching in tree-shadow as his eyes and ears scoured the timber. Further into the trees, he heard the faint, muffled snorting of the horses. Then a slower, shifting movement, as a heavy-framed man edged awkwardly closer through the pines. Anderson sighted the man's face as a white blur in the darkness, the black shirt blending his figure in with the shadows. The dark man smiled tightly, easing the carbine to a firmer grip in his hands. Grierson might be a killer with his fists, but he wasn't cut out to be sneaking around at night. This time, it was Anderson who had the edge.

He waited until the thickset *hombre* lurched past the tree where he crouched in hiding, and pushed lithely up from the ground on the soles of his moccasined feet.

'Mister Grierson?' the dark man murmured.

The burly prizefighter spun hurriedly round as the words were spoken, struggling to bring his pistol into line. Anderson had the carbine reversed, waiting for the move. Butt-end of the Winchester slammed into the prizefighter's face, connected solidly with his jaw. Grierson went down hard and heavy as a lopped oak, crashing to the dirt. The gun dropped unfired from his hand, skidding towards Anderson, who bent and gathered up the weapon. The dark man stowed the pistol in his belt, and turned the carbine around to level it on the prone figure of Grierson. He needn't have bothered, the prizefighter was out cold, his jaw already darkened by an ugly bruise. Couldn't have done better if he'd learned the ring trade himself, Anderson decided. For some reason, the thought made him smile.

He rolled the stunned roughneck over, using Grierson's bandanna to bind both arms behind him at the wrists. For the moment, he made no effort to gag the thickset man. Way he saw it, Grierson would be a while before he felt like calling out to anyone else. Anderson dragged the unconscious man into deeper shadow by the roots of the pine and left him there, going forward more warily through the trees with the carbine lined ahead. Seemed like friend Copeland had arranged a reception committee for him, after all. Maybe he'd better find out who else was in on the play.

Up ahead the tethered animals snorted again, one of them breaking into a shrill, whinnying sound. Anderson slowed his pace, edging carefully from one tree bole to the next as his eyes raked the darkness in front. Catching sight of fresh movement some thirty yards or so away, he halted and pressed flat to the first trunk he met.

'Grierson? That you?' The words carried to him as a hoarse, uncertain whisper. A tall, slim shape detached itself from the surrounding trees, moving cautiously past the ponderosa clump where he stayed hidden. Anderson's keen eyes defined the outline of Lon Mather, his gun already drawn and held level on the trees in front. The dark man eased stealthily around the far side of the pine bole, and in behind him, bringing the Winchester into line.

Mather was a gunhawk, and not a tracker. All the same he was quick to sense the shift of movement behind him, and whipped around swift as a mountain cat, ready to shoot as he turned. He almost made it, but not quite. Anderson lashed the carbine barrel hard against the gunman's wrist, jarring the pistol from his hold. Mather gasped in pain, and tried to grab the barrel of the Winchester, but Anderson stood clear as the pistol fell, and brought up the muzzle of the .45-70 to level on the tall man's chin.

'One smart move, an' I blow your goddamn head off,' Anderson told him. 'Now take me to them horses, Mather, an' no tricks.'

'How about my gun?' The blond man still winced, massaging his hammered wrist.

'Leave it lyin'. You won't be needin' it.' Anderson stepped back, gesturing with the carbine muzzle 'Now turn around, an' start walkin'. An' don't worry yourself none over Grierson. He's out of the play.'

119

'I aim to remember this, Anderson,' Lon Mather said. He stood motionless for an instant, his pale bleached eyes fixing Anderson with a stare so cold and pitiless it sent a shiver like icewater down the dark man's spine.

'Figured you might,' Anderson smiled amiably, glad to be on the right side of the Winchester. 'Now do like I tell you, and I might stay friendly.'

Mather swore thickly, and turned, going back the way he'd come. Anderson followed three or four feet behind, keeping himself out of the tall man's reach while still too close to miss his shot. Nobody else met up with them, and after a while they reached the clump of trees where the horses waited. The animals didn't wait alone. Ross Copeland was there, leaning back against the nearest of the pine trunks as he smoked one of his long cigars. On seeing Mather step out from the timber he frowned uncertainly, his thin foxy face puzzled for once. When he glimpsed the second man behind him the rancher let fall the cigar, his right hand thrusting swiftly inside the Prince Albert coat.

'Try it, an' you'll be sorry,' Anderson warned him. He stood with his carbine covering Copeland and Mather together, his Indian features merciless. 'What I got here makes a hole you can put your fist in, an' it don't improve your health at all. Now pitch out the stingy gun, an' git them hands lifted.'

Copeland studied the Winchester muzzle for the fraction of a second before he complied, throwing down the gun. Pocket-sized pistol from the look of it, Anderson decided. He motioned Mather to join the rancher by the tree, and moved in closer with the carbine levelled on them.

'Real nice of you to wait out here for me, Mister Copeland.' The dark man was smiling again, the kind of smile a wolf might find before closing in on his prey. 'Sure do appreciate it, an' that's the truth.' He nodded towards the tall, stooping figure of Mather, who still held his bruised wrist. 'Told you I met better'n him in my time. He could outdraw me, sure, but fast shootin' ain't everythin', or prizefightin' neither. Ask your friend Grierson once he wakes up again.'

'Don't crow too soon, Anderson.' Copeland had regained some of his composure. His icy tone matched the chill green of his eyes, that showed as jade slivers in the narrow, yellowish face. 'Maybe you fooled Hatch, but we know better. Curt Fisher ran down your tracks later on, led us to the horses. You can't buck all of us, breed, the organization is too big for you to take on. And once we've dealt with you, we can take our time removing Galvan.'

'Is that right?' Anderson caught the unease of the tethered horses, the set of the heads and ears that pointed away to his left. 'OK, Copeland. Call out your friend yonder, or this

121

Winchester is liable to go off.'

'Come on out, Nate!' Copeland seemed to have lost his earlier nervousness, the green eyes sly and calculating as he sang out to the man in cover. 'Come on, you hear? He has us at gunpoint!'

'You bet I have.' Anderson cut a rapid glance to the left as the undergrowth shook and burst open. The short, heavyset *hombre* he remembered as Nathan Coe stepped out cautiously, leading a string of horses by their halter-ropes. In that sudden, swift glimpse Anderson counted the animals that followed. There were six of them.

Off to his right fresh movement flickered and Curt Fisher heaved upward from the thick undergrowth, hoisting his gun for the shot. Anderson swung the Winchester for him as the others rushed him, hearing too late the hurried clip of low-heeled boots at his back.

He was still lining up on Fisher when the gunbarrel slammed down across his skull, taking him forward into darkness.

*   *   *

Somebody was hammering a handspike through his head, he figured. It was made of fire and ice and burned and chilled him by turns, and whoever was hammering it had to be taking his time and doing a thorough job. Anderson groaned and opened his eyes, the pain threatening to slice the top off his skull. He lay back, waiting for the worst of the pangs to ebb from him as the room lurched about him to right itself.

'Glad you could join us, Anderson,' Copeland sounded amused. The rancher sat in the tall, heavy-backed chair across from him, smiling as he lit another cigar. The derby hat hung from a peg on the wall, the black Prince Albert beside it, and the light from the oil-lamp shone dully on his fox-red hair. As though from a huge distance, Anderson took in the sight of the thin, angular figure in its grey vest and flannel pants, the striped shirt with its sleeve-garters. 'Say hello to our guest, fellers.'

Laughter that answered was mocking, and rang harshly against his skull. Anderson grimaced, tried vainly to move. He was roped to the heavy-backed chair where he'd been seated to face Copeland, and the knots were so tight he figured he'd have no circulation left in a while. He scanned the room about him as his vision cleared, noting the table topped with green baize, the cues and stacked balls. He saw, too, the men who laughed, and who now crowded the room about him. Mather and Coe to his right, and on the far side Fisher and a big, florid-faced man in a broadcloth coat and silk vest. Over by the door leaned the tall, heavyset figure of Walsh Hindman, grinning through his blue-black stubble. The one he'd forgotten, back in the timber. Only Grierson didn't laugh.

123

The thickset prizefighter slouched in a chair by the billiard table, scowling and nursing his jaw. Right now, Anderson gained some pleasure from the sight. Trouble was, he got the feeling he was about to pay for it before long.

'You've met most of my business associates, I believe.' Copeland grinned tightly, drew the cigar away to breathe smoke-rings at the ceiling. 'I felt that the billiard-room was an appropriate location for our little tête-à-tête. I'd say our encounters have had a touch of sport about them—a game of chance, perhaps. It's a game that can have only one winner, Anderson.' Watching the dark man grit his teeth as the pain returned, he smiled wider, tucking the cigar in the corner of his mouth. 'Once your headache has cleared, we can discuss matters more reasonably, don't you think?'

'Know who I owe for that, anyhow.' Anderson bit out the words through the pain of the handspike in his skull. The dark man looked to the tall, grinning figure of Hindman by the door, his grey eyes flinty and cold. 'Ain't nothin' new for you, is it, Walsh? Reckon you're a regular hand for sneakin' up back of a man, an' no mistake.'

'Shut your mouth, breed!' Hindman's grin vanished, wiped away in a moment. The big, stubble-faced saloonman pushed clear of the door, starting in for Anderson with both fists clenching. 'Oughta kill you here an' now, you half-Injun bastard!'

'Like you did Espinoza, huh?' Anderson didn't try hiding the contempt in his voice. He met the other's muddy gaze without flinching, bracing himself in readiness for a blow as Hindman closed in. 'At least Mather shot Gomez from the front, an' he didn't need five bullets, neither!'

'That'll do, Walsh!' Copeland's sharp command halted Hindman before he reached the man in the chair. 'Back against the door, and stay put.' He waited as the scowling saloonman gave back to his former position in the doorway, turned his green stare on Anderson. 'You appear to be more perceptive than you look, my friend. Perhaps you'd care to enlighten us as to what you know?'

'You planted Espinoza at the Galvan ranch,' Anderson told him, then ploughed on doggedly, flinching a little at the jagged pain in his head. 'That gave you a man on the inside, who could report back to you should you need it. An' Espinoza was a ladies' man, too. I reckon you set him to make a play for Mrs Galvan, knowin' it'd raise Diego's hackles agin him. Maybe you figured on gettin' yourself a murder that way.'

'Not quite.' Copeland studied his prisoner reprovingly, shaking his foxy head. 'Such a method would leave too much to chance, after all. Espinoza was a useful spy, and we felt that his—natural inclinations, shall we say—would

125

lead him into conflict with Galvan. This would provide us with a motive for murder only. What we had to do was ensure that the killing took place, and obtain the murder weapon.'

'That's one thing I ain't figured.' Anderson fought briefly against the constricting ropes and gave up, relaxing as best he could. 'How'd you git him to steal the pistol from the house, huh? What was the story?'

'Simple enough. A robbery,' Copeland chuckled, breathing out a fresh plume of cigar-smoke. 'No harm in telling you, Anderson. You won't be talking, after all. Espinoza was told that he and two of my men were to stage a robbery on the bank in Galesboro, and leave the gun behind to throw blame on Galvan. He was to steal the pistol, which from the information he gave us was a distinctive weapon, and meet the others in the timber at the border between ourselves and the JD ranch.'

'An' Walsh here was once constable in Galesboro, right?' Anderson eyed the big man unforgivingly as he spoke.

'As you say, my friend.' The rancher eyed his cigar appreciatively, returned it to his mouth. 'We made some pretence of checking out the place in readiness, but the robbery was never contemplated. All we needed was Espinoza, and the gun. By this time, of course, he had become too involved with Mrs Galvan, and had come close to death at her husband's

126

hands. He had outlived his usefulness, you understand.'

'Sure do.' Anderson shook his head, disgust plain in his voice. 'Dumb son had served his purpose, an' it was time he helped you put a rope round Diego's neck! With friends like you, Copeland, he never stood a chance.'

'He was a fool, too greedy for his own good.' Copeland swept his free hand in a gesture of dismissal, his narrow face impatient. 'He didn't just want his cut, he had to have the woman too! We asked him to seduce the bitch, not fall for her, damn it. Once he got himself in too deep, he was no use to us.'

'Maybe.' Anderson's look stayed flinty as it rested on the rancher. 'Meantime, I'd be obliged if you didn't use that kind of a name for Mrs Galvan. Either that, or wash out your mouth with soap first chance that comes.'

'Don't tell me what to say in my own ranchhouse, breed,' Ross Copeland said.

He got out of the chair and leaned forward, slapping the bound man hard across the face with his open hand. Force of it drove Anderson's head back, and he felt the heavy dress ring Copeland wore gash the half-healed cut on his lip. Copeland backhanded him on the other side of the face, and stepped back, lowering both hands as he smiled again.

'Just a reminder.' The red-haired man replaced the cigar in his mouth, settled himself back in the chair. 'Individualism such as yours
127

has its merits, my friend, but there are occasions when it requires a little discipline. I trust you understand the lesson?'

Anderson nodded, aware of the sluggish trickle of blood that ran down his chin.

'So far you've guessed pretty well at our methods.' Copeland grinned coldly around the cigar butt, his green eyes holding a light of amusement. 'Suppose you tell us how the murder itself was carried out. I'm sure we'd all like to hear.'

'Simple enough.' Anderson paused, spitting blood from his torn mouth to stain the rancher's carpet. His grey stare held with Copeland as he spoke. 'Espinoza met your two men in the timber like you said, and handed over the gun. One feller kept him talkin'—not too tall, an' kind of slim, wearin' high-heel boots. Like Fisher, let's say. Other *hombre* was big an' wore low-heel townsman's boots. He turned the gun on Espinoza, an' emptied it into his back.'

'And who might the killer be?' Copeland's smile had tightened a notch, the hand clenched around the cigar.

'Already told you that.' Anderson glanced to the man by the door, and framed a bloodstained smile of his own. 'Walsh Hindman has the build, an' he's wearin' the boots. Then again, he ain't no gunfighter worth the name.' He broke off, switching his glance to the tall, gangling figure of Lon Mather to his

128

right. 'No way it could have been Mather here, for instance. Apart from he ain't heavy enough to leave the prints I found, he'd shoot from the front an' once, I reckon. That ain't Walsh's style.' He smiled wider, tasting blood as the hammers rang inside his head. 'Walsh has to be the only backshooter so dumb he'd empty five slugs into a feller stood so close he could be powder-burned.'

He watched as Hindman started forward again, letting the smile die as Copeland signed to the saloonman to stay put. Walsh Hindman obeyed, his stubbled face dark with rage.

'After that, they bundled him on his horse an' dumped him at the line shack.' The bound man in the chair spoke stonily, his look coming back to Copeland again. 'I found the tracks, Copeland, an' they tell a good story. Trouble with givin' that kind of a job to amateurs is they ain't never careful enough. Fisher an' Hindman was in such a rush to git away they didn't rub out their prints too well. Once I followed them into the timber, it was real easy.'

'I see.' Copeland spared a venomous glance for his two hirelings, chill stare of his eyes hushing the excuses in their throats. 'You're a smart man, Anderson, I have to admit. Not smart enough, however. You'll be taking your knowledge with you to a place where no one else will hear it, believe me.'

'You reckon I'm so dumb I wouldn't tell nobody else?' Anderson asked.

He waited out the shocked moment of silence that followed, keeping his eyes level with Copeland's as the rancher frowned for the first time.

'You heard me, Copeland.' Anderson tried not to think too hard about what they had in mind for him after this discussion in the billiard-room. Somehow, he managed to keep his voice steady. 'Diego knows it, an' Josefa too. Last I heard she was aimin' to tell Sheriff Hatch all about it, once she got to Hillsburg.'

'My God, Ross!' From left of the seated Copeland the big, broadcloth-coated figure broke into speech, the words leaving him in a cry of anguish. Rutherford grabbed the rancher by the shoulder, his florid moustached features gleaming wet in the light of the oil lamp. 'If what he says is true, we're finished! I warned you against these murders from the beginning, Ross. I said you'd gone too far. In heaven's name, what are we to do?'

'Pull yourself together, Gene!' Copeland rounded sharply on the taller man, tugging his shoulder from the other's grasp. 'You were eager enough to come in with me when there was the chance of money and a circuit judge's job at the end of it. You've all the greed it takes, and none of the guts. Now do something useful and keep out of this, you hear?'

'If you say so, Ross.' Rutherford mopped with a silk handkerchief at his fleshy, sweating face. Looking to Anderson, his sad eyes pleaded. 'I had nothing to do with the murders, Anderson, I swear. I should never have been a party to this business, I see now. It's going to be the ruin of me...'

'Shut up, Gene!' The red-haired man cut him short, still studying Anderson through those chill green eyes. 'I must say I'm beginning to weary of this interview, Anderson. It seems you've already told us most of what you know.'

'How 'bout you ask him where Galvan is hid?' Lon Mather suggested.

He didn't move from where he stood to Anderson's right, flexing his bruised wrist carefully. Deep in the weathered, old-mannish face the bleached-blue eyes gave no hint of pity, or any other emotion, scanning the bound figure of Anderson as a cat might watch a sparrow with a broken wing.

'Reckon he'd tell you, if you asked him nice, Mister Copeland.'

'No need, Lon.' The rancher shook his fox-red head, relaxing as the smile returned. 'I think we know where to begin looking for Galvan without any help from Anderson.' He paused, tapping ash from the cigar into a metal tray placed by the arm of his chair as his glance went over the prisoner once more. 'You have been our problem, Anderson. It's clear that we have underestimated you, but that no longer matters. Once you have been disposed of, Galvan will be helpless, and when he and his wife are found your evidence will disappear. I think we may call on Mrs Galvan early tomorrow morning, boys. No doubt she will be glad to see us.'

'You leave her be, Copeland!' Anderson shouted, ignoring the ache in his skull as he fought the ropes. 'She ain't done nothin' to you, damn it!'

He saw the green stare freeze over, and for a moment felt sick.

'I shall do as I choose, Anderson,' Ross Copeland told him. 'You, my friend, will be too dead to prevent it.' He puffed out cigar-smoke, chuckling softly. 'You have impressed us with your powers of detection, but I wonder if you are aware of our true purpose. Have you, for instance, any idea why I should have purchased this land, and made offers for the properties of Galvan and Hernandez?'

'Ain't cattle-ranchin', I worked that one out.' Anderson wasn't thinking too hard about the question, his mind still troubled at the thought of Josefa in the hands of Copeland and his bunch. 'Seems to me it don't leave too much else, other than minin', maybe.'

'There you have it,' the redhead nodded, his eyes still holding the same cold amusement. 'Some time ago, Anderson, my employers in Chicago commissioned a geological survey of land already purchased to the north of here. The survey revealed a solid wedge of valuable mineral deposits that continued southwards to where we are now.' He paused, letting the

132

information sink in, before continuing. 'The word from our surveyor was that the strata containing these deposits extends across the land occupied by this ranch, and the holdings of Galvan and Hernandez. Since purchasing my own property, I've had boreholes sunk and soundings taken, and I can now assure you that the surveyor was correct. This stretch of the Pecos Valley is a treasure-house, just waiting to be opened. What have you to say to that, my friend?'

'Not much, I guess.' Suddenly Anderson seemed to feel the full weight of his weariness, the pain that threatened to burst his head apart. 'Reckon that accounts for the murders, an' all your other tricks. With somethin' like that in mind, you could afford to pay Mather here too.'

'Do you really think we'd allow someone like you to stand in our way?' Copeland's voice sounded almost pitying. Almost. 'You picked the wrong man for a friend in Diego Galvan, Anderson. From the moment you came north to help him, you were finished.' He sat up suddenly, crushing out the cigar on the metal tray beside him. 'I think we've spent enough time discussing this, Anderson. You're quite an amusing fellow in your way, but the conversation has begun to pall, I'm afraid.'

'Ross, for God's sake!' Rutherford pleaded with the rancher, his red face awash with sweat. 'Please, not another murder! Ross, I beg you…'

'He hardly leaves us the choice, does he, Gene?' Copeland didn't turn his head.

'I had no idea this was going to happen.' Rutherford glanced hopelessly at the hard-faced men around him, a trapped look in his eyes. 'You know I only came here when you asked me to bring the accounts from the office. I never expected to be involved in a murder, like this…'

'That's your misfortune, damn it!' Copeland's voice cracked harshly as the rancher lost patience. The redhead turned on Rutherford, anger flaring in the tight-planed features. 'You're no use to us here, that's obvious. Pick up the books and get out, and make sure you don't miss anything. I'll handle this side of things.'

Rutherford nodded hastily, struggling vainly to speak through the fear that choked him. The lawyer grabbed up the valise that stood on the carpet beside him, and all but ran by Walsh Hindman to disappear out of the door.

'That saves us one problem,' Copeland muttered. He glanced back to the tall, half-stooped figure of Lon Mather. 'Lon, I think you'd better take Anderson outside.'

'Guess not, Mister Copeland.' Mather shook his cropped blond head, pale eyes studying Anderson with the same lack of feeling. 'This kind of killin' ain't my style.'

134

'You're on my payroll, goddamn it!' Voice of the rancher cut at him, matched by the vicious stare of the eyes. Mather seemed not to hear it, his own face expressionless.

'For now, maybe.' The tall gunhawk didn't sound too impressed. 'You hired me as a gunhand, Mister Copeland, not a backshooter. I'll kill men for you, sure, as long as the judge rules self-defence. Ain't in no hurry to put my neck inside a noose, an' that's a fact.'

'I shall be a long time forgetting this, Mather,' Copeland told him.

'Have it your way,' the blond man shrugged, one hand resting easily on the Schofield pistol in its holster. Mather scanned the faces around him, found no one willing to meet his gaze. 'Some things a man kin do, others he cain't have no part of. I built me a reputation over the years, Mister Copeland, an' I aim to keep it. Once this here business is through, I take my cut an' head out of New Mexico. OK?'

'If that's the way you want it.' Copeland forced the words through his gritted teeth. Abruptly, the rancher swung away from the gunman, looking to where Grierson still slumped in the chair. 'Hal, get up out of there. I'm counting on you to take care of Anderson for me.'

'It'll be a pleasure, boss.' The prizefighter loomed to his feet, scowling still as he massaged the bruise on his chin. 'Sonofabitch nearly busted my jaw, I reckon.'

135

'Take Nathan with you.' Copeland nodded to the stocky, bearded man, who also moved closer. 'Cut him loose, and take him somewhere away from here before you kill him.' He halted for a moment, his cold stare fixing on both men in turn. 'No mistakes, Hal. Understand?'

'You betcha.' Grierson's look shifted to the bound figure of Anderson, and he grinned unpleasantly. 'This time I'll make real sure, boss. That's a promise.'

He stayed watching Anderson and rubbing his injured jaw as Coe moved around behind the prisoner, drawing a knife from the sheath on his belt. The blade cut through the tightly knotted ropes, and Anderson howled with pain, collapsing forward as the blood rushed back through his numbed limbs. Coe let him fall, and the dark man sprawled face down on the carpet, groaning as pain and circulation returned together.

'Don't worry, Anderson.' From above him, Ross Copeland spoke, his voice bare of pity. 'After a while, you won't feel anything.' Down on the ground, Anderson saw the booted feet turn from him as the rancher called out to Grierson. 'Hal, get him out of here!'

'Sure thing, Mister Copeland.' Grierson took a bruising grip on the arm of the fallen man, dragging him upright. Coe moved in to seize Anderson from the left, both men hanging tight as they hauled their prisoner

136

towards the door. 'Git movin', you half-Injun bastard!'

Dragging along with both feet trailing to ruck up the carpet, Anderson caught a last glimpse of the men in the room who stood to watch him go. Tall, impassive Lon Mather, Curt Fisher with his face set into a sneer of triumph, Copeland's foxy, slyly mocking smile. Walsh Hindman was last, closest to the door as they hauled Anderson by him. The big saloonman grinned, raking him over with merciless, mud-brown eyes. 'Solong, breed,' Hindman told him.

The dark man had no time to answer, Grierson and Coe pulling him out through the door, their grip putting fresh bruises in his flesh as they lugged him like a sack. Heading along the corridor that led outside, Anderson decided he'd finally played and lost. Maybe he wasn't going to be pulled out of this hole he'd dug for himself.

He tried not to think too hard about what was still to come.

CHAPTER EIGHT

He rode forward through the trees, wincing a little at the throbbing in his head. His unbound arms still seared with pain, and his battered body felt like it had lost a battle with a

137

threshing machine, but Anderson figured these were the least of his worries. Like Copeland had reminded him, in a while they wouldn't trouble him at all. He held the black on a short rein, keeping the animal to a walk as the other two followed. Grierson and Coe rode close behind him to left and right, each man with his pistol levelled. Too far off to be reached by a desperate spring, but well within range for a killing shot. Anderson sighed, grimaced as his skull rang like an echo. These two might not be in Mather's class, or his own, but right now they held all the aces. To try jumping them in this situation was no better than suicide.

Then again, it might not make too much difference.

He breathed out harshly, the memory of his own mistakes coming back to haunt him. All along he'd figured he was so goddamn smart, and where had it got him? He'd let himself be caught and worked over not once, but twice, by a bunch of gunhawks that—Mather apart—he ought to have been able to outwit easily. And now he was riding to his death, while Diego and Josefa were in as much danger as they'd ever been. Anderson groaned at the memory, shaking his head. Maybe he'd been too old to take on a job like this, after all. What was the use that he knew all about the murders, and Copeland's plans, now that it was too late?

Copeland was a tricky son of a bitch, he had to admit that much. Way the rancher had used

Hindman and Fisher to kill Espinoza had been smart thinking, all right. It gave him a further hold over his choice as future county sheriff, and tied Walsh in too tight to break loose, unless he was pining for a rope around his neck. Same time it rid Copeland of someone who had become a nuisance, and framed Diego for the killing. As murders went, they didn't come much neater than that. And now he had Rutherford in another kind of armlock, that he could make count for plenty once the lawyer made circuit judge. Copeland had it all figured, sure enough. Anderson had shaken him up for a while, but that was all. A few more well-placed murders, and the foxy bastard would be set to take over all this part of the Pecos Valley.

Heading deeper into the timber, he scowled and shook off the thought, a last spurt of anger rising. The hell with it, he wasn't dead yet! It was getting on for morning already, and by now Diego must have guessed that something was wrong. Maybe Josefa too. Could be they weren't far away, and looking for him. And if they were around, it was a poor way for him to thank them, giving up hope too early.

Anderson drew a deep breath, felt the ache in his head as the breath was released. Hell of a big if, all the same, the dark man told himself.

'OK, Anderson!' Harsh voice of Grierson halted him, halfway through the timber stand. 'That oughta be far enough, I reckon!'

Anderson reined in the black stallion,

glanced back to where the gunhands followed with their weapons lined on him. He saw the ugly, lopsided grin the prizefighter gave him, and figured that maybe he'd run out of time, after all.

'Git down from the hoss, breed!' The thickset *hombre* was enjoying himself, the pain of his punished jaw forgotten for the moment. Grierson nodded sharply to the rider on Anderson's far side. 'Keep him covered, Nate, you hear?'

Coe grunted some muffled sound that went missing in the thick beard. Seemed like whatever else he was good at, it didn't include speech. Right now, though, he had no need of words as he kept the pistol's foresight level with a point between Anderson's shoulders. No chance for anything heroic here, the dark man figured. He climbed down from the black and let the trail-rope drop, hearing Grierson step down behind him.

'That's fine, *hombre*. Just fine.' The prizefighter didn't improve his looks when he was happy. With that grin on his face, Grierson put Anderson in mind of a gargoyle he'd seen on a mission church in Old Mexico one time, and they didn't come any uglier than that. 'OK, Nate, you kin git down now. I got him covered.'

He stood with both feet planted firm in his fighter's balanced crouch, the heavy Colt levelled on Anderson's middle. He had

Anderson's own .45 Army stowed in his belt, the dark man noticed, maybe as a reminder of how things had turned around since their run-in the night before. Anderson let the thought occupy him for a fragment of a second as Nathan Coe swung down from his saddle to join them.

'Looks like the finish, breed, don't it?' Grierson's voice held a vicious mockery. The bulky, black-shirted gunman studied Anderson carefully over the pistol sight, turning the possibilities in his mind. 'Boss didn't say nothin' 'bout makin' it quick, Anderson. Long as you end up dead, he ain't gonna worry too much, I reckon.' He grinned across to Coe, who bared stained teeth in an unwholesome leer that rent the mass of beard. 'What d'you think, Nate? Shall I put a slug through his feet first, or his legs? Or maybe a little higher, huh? That oughta be worth a try.'

He lined up the weapon on Anderson's groin, squinting along the sight towards his target. The dark man gritted his teeth as he faced the gun, fighting to stay upright and motionless as sweat broke from the roots of his hair, and stung into his eyes.

'Drop the *pistola, cabron*!' Another voice said.

It came from dense timber away to the left, and the sound of it froze Grierson for that instant. Almost as the words were spoken, Anderson heard the ferocious snarling and

141

baying of dogs, and two huge mastiffs came charging out of the undergrowth. The dark man threw himself flat as Hal Grierson swung away from him, firing wildly in the direction of the voice. Far side of him, Nate Coe had the chance for only a single shot, triggered in panic as the dogs rushed him. Fear made him hurry, misjudging his aim, and the bullet sang high over their heads to splatter bark from a tree beyond. Next minute the mastiffs had him down, the three of them rolling and snarling and howling together in a tangled heap. Grierson was wavering between sending a second shot into the trees or into Anderson when guns crashed from the timber, and a slug tore the black hat from his head. Grierson froze once again, standing as if rooted with the gun held out in front of him.

'*Abajo con su pistola, cabron!*' Voice from the thicket bit keener than before, hard and merciless. 'Drop the gun, you rat's leavings, and quickly! *Sabe usted?*'

Vicious lash of the command broke Hal Grierson from his trance. The prizefighter flung the pistol away from him as though the metal burned him, hurrying to raise both hands in the air.

'Don't shoot, feller!' Grierson pleaded. 'Don't kill me, mister. I ain't done nothin'.'

Coe and the dogs were still milling around on the floor as Anderson got to his feet, looking about him. From what he could make of the churning mass of human and canine life in the leaf mould, Coe was taking a beating, and it didn't seem to bother Anderson at all. He picked up the gun that the bearded man had let fall in the struggle, as Raul Nunez dashed out from the trees, shouting as he ran. '*Cristobal! Mateo! Aqui, perros! Aqui, pronto!*'

Hearing his voice, the mastiffs let go their victim and stood off him, growling thickly in their throats. Raul nodded curtly to Anderson, and bent to gather up the pistol that Grierson had thrown away. Behind him, Diego Galvan and Martin Quiroga stepped out from the shelter of the trees, the younger man leading three horses by their halter-ropes. Seeing Anderson, both men grinned, coming forward.

'Good to see you, fellers,' the dark man told them. He turned back to Raul Nunez, who now stood covering both disarmed gunmen with his looted pistol. 'This is the second time I am in your debt, Raul. *Mil gracias.*'

'*Por nada, señor.*' The oldster's withered face didn't change expression. 'The *señora* wished us to ensure your safety, and we have done as she asked, no more.'

'Sure as hell grateful to you, all the same.' Anderson glanced to where Nate Coe had struggled to a sitting position, moaning and clasping his bitten right arm. He and Grierson looked a whole lot less impressive than they had a few moments back. Now the bearded *hombre* pleaded with him, seemingly

143

recovering his powers of speech.

'Anderson, I'm bitten all to hell here,' Coe whimpered like a thrashed pup, wary still of the mastiffs who growled only yards away. 'Damn it, I'm bleeding ... I could die...'

'You will not die, *cabron*,' Diego told him. He spared the fallen man a brief glance, the hawkish features showing their contempt. 'Unfortunately, you will live to rot in a cell, I think.' He left the moaning gunman lying, instead moving on to where Hal Grierson stood, scared and trembling under the threat of the guns held by Raul and Martin. Galvan eyed the thickset man for a moment, turned to the youngster. 'This is the one you spoke of, who paid insults to Josefa?'

Martin Quiroga nodded.

'Now just a minute, mister...' Grierson began.

He got no further. Diego Galvan punched him hard in his mouth, force of the blow knocking him to the ground. Grierson grunted and sat up, spitting blood and busted teeth. For a while he stayed there, one hand clasped to his aching jaw as he stared fearfully down the barrel of Galvan's pistol.

'OK, Diego!' Anderson was hard tasked not to smile. 'He's taken enough, I reckon.'

He moved over to the fallen man, tugging the .45 Army out of Grierson's belt. Beside him, Diego Galvan glared down at the terrified prizefighter, his pistol still levelled.

144

'Cross me again, *hombre*, and I will kill you,' the Mexican said. He gestured with the gun, his voice harshening. 'Now roll over, and lie on your face.'

Grierson complied, his face ashen as he waited for a slug in the back of his head. Galvan signed to Martin, who drew a set of rawhide thongs from his jacket, and used them to secure Grierson's hands behind his back. Beyond them, Raul Nunez tore strips from Nate Coe's grubby undershirt, bandaging the worst of the bites. Galvan left the youngster to watch Grierson, and walked back to where Anderson stood waiting with the two guns in his hands.

'*Buenos dias*, Andres.' The rancher eyed the battered figure of his friend, his gaunt face frowning at sight of the bruises. 'They have hurt you much, *amigo*?'

'Not so it shows.' Anderson touched gingerly at the swollen bruise on his skull. He could get used to being alive, given time, he figured. 'How come you found me here?'

'After a time, we knew something was wrong,' Diego told him. The big Mexican replaced the spent loads in the old Griswold and Grier pistol, slid the weapon into its holster. 'Teofilo would have come to find you, but I was less sure, and felt it better to wait. Then Martin and Raul arrived, with the dogs. Josefa sent them for you as soon as she reached the ranch. She sent also for the sheriff, but he

145

may only just have reached Hillsburg, and it is possible he has not yet received her message.' He paused, his dark eyes studying the other man more closely. 'Martin tells me that she was here, and that you spoke to her. *Verdad?*'

'That's right.' Anderson met the Mexican's stare as levelly as he could. 'Reckon she come lookin' for you, *amigo*. Was me told her to go back. So what happened after that, if you don't mind me askin'?'

'We followed your tracks to the ranch-house, the dogs helped us.' Galvan glanced to where the mastiffs crouched in the grass, still eyeing Coe intently. 'We were ready to attack the place itself, but saw these two bring you outside. Afterwards, it was simple to take another route, and head them off.'

'Yeah.' Anderson thought about the grinning face of Grierson, the pistol muzzle lined on his groin. 'Good thing you arrived when you did, *amigo*.' He halted as a sudden thought struck him. 'You saw Rutherford leave?'

'Rutherford? *Si*, he drove off just before you, he will not be far from here.' Galvan frowned at him, puzzled for the moment. 'Why do you ask, my friend?'

'Best we should catch up with him, Diego,' Anderson told the Mexican. 'From what I heard at the ranch-house, he could be headed some place to destroy evidence. Seems Copeland wants your land an' Teofilo's for minin', *amigo*. What's under that grass is worth more'n what you're grazin' cattle on, so he tells me anyhow.'

'And Espinoza?' Galvan once more eyed his friend carefully as he questioned.

'Walsh Hindman killed him, on Copeland's orders. Curt Fisher was in on it, too.' The dark man holstered the pistol, stuck the other weapon in his belt. 'Let's go, Diego. Ain't got too much time, I reckon.'

'Martin!' Galvan called out to the youngster behind him. 'Mount, and come with us. Raul, stand guard on these *ladrones* with your dogs until we return!'

'At once, Señor Galvan!' Martin sheathed his gun, running for his mount. Raul nodded gravely, and settled on his haunches, patting the nearest of his mastiffs as his pistol covered the two captured gunmen. Anderson took a parting look at the dismounted group, and went over to the black horse, mounting up as Galvan and Martin rode over to join him. The dogs were still growling softly as the three riders left them, heading away through the trees.

They didn't have much trouble finding Rutherford. His one-horse buggy wasn't built to drive anywhere off the main trails, and the road he took was longer, allowing them plenty of time. Cutting across country and avoiding the main stage route with its detours, the three horsemen ran their mounts down a brushy

147

slope on to the road, and were waiting there when the buggy rounded the last bend and came into sight.

'Hold it, Rutherford' Anderson called. 'We want to talk to you.'

He sat the black stallion in the middle of the trail, the .45 Colt Army lined on the man in the buggy seat. Rutherford hauled on the traces, and the vehicle slewed to a halt in a smothering cloud of dust. Through the hanging pall the red, moustached face of the lawyer stared at him, shiny with sweat and wide-eyed in terror.

'What do you want from me?' Rutherford's voice quivered, his big hands shaking on the reins. The lawyer scanned the hard-faced Mexicans on either side, brought his gaze back again to the dark man who held him at gunpoint. 'Anderson, I swear to you I had nothing to do with those killings. It was all Copeland's idea, believe me!'

'If you tell it that way in court, I might.' Anderson's voice was cold as a frozen creek. 'Right now, we ain't got time to hear it. Throw out the valise!'

'Anderson.' The lawyer eyed his captor uncertainly, licking his lips. 'I'm not sure this is appropriate, in the circumstances. This is confidential information...'

'Not any more it ain't!' Anderson flipped the gunbarrel sharply, growing impatient. 'Throw it down, Rutherford, an' make it fast!'

Rutherford stared down the muzzle of the

148

gun, and nodded. The lawyer reached into the buggy, and hurled the valise clear. The loaded bag landed in the trail and burst open, papers scattering across the ground. Anderson holstered the .45 Army and climbed down, gathering up the books and loose sheets as Martin kept the sweating Rutherford at gunpoint. The dark man squatted in the road, the records on his lap as he flicked through the pages.

'Some interestin' accounts you got here, Mister Rutherford.' Anderson studied the open book in front of him, his lean face growing a wintry smile. 'Lon Mather, one thousand dollars for services rendered. Walsh Hindman, seven hundred dollars fifty for services rendered.' He paused, glancing up to the man in the buggy. 'Sounds kind of unspecific, don't it—services rendered? Hell of a drinks bill, wouldn't you say?'

'This is hardly the place to discuss such matters, Mister Anderson.' The lawyer struggled to regain his lost self-assurance. The shake in the voice, though, gave him away. 'On behalf of my client, I must protest...'

'You ain't in court now, Rutherford. Save it for later.' Anderson flipped the pages, searching the entries as they showed. 'Now here's what I call real interestin', fellers. Five hundred dollars to Manuel Espinoza for services rendered, an' it ain't no more'n a month old.' He gave a sidelong look to where

Diego Galvan sat his horse, frowning grimly at the lawyer. 'Way I heard it, he was workin' at the JD, Diego. That right?'

'*Verdad*, Andres.' The former gunfighter grated the words, his eyes never leaving Rutherford as he spoke.

'Seems kind of funny for Copeland to be payin' him that amount of *dinero*, don't you reckon?' Anderson scanned the entry one more time, and closed the book, hugging the documents to him as he got to his feet. The dark man crammed them into the valise, forced the bulging container shut. 'Judge ought to find plenty to interest him in this little haul, Rutherford. You an' your friend Copeland are finished in New Mexico, better believe it.'

Rutherford didn't answer him, sitting slump-shouldered in the buggy seat. The lawyer's florid face had lost its colour for the moment, the shock of Anderson's discovery turning him white as a corpse. Any other time, the dark man might have felt pity for him. Right now, though, he figured he had none to spare.

'That takes care of the evidence,' Anderson told the waiting Mexicans. He walked back to the vehicle and swung the heavy valise back inside, grunting with the effort. 'Reckon it kin rest up there for now, unless Mister Rutherford here figures on makin' a run. An' you weren't thinkin' of doin' that, were you, Rutherford?'

150

'If he tries, he will travel with a bullet in his belly,' Martin Quiroga said.

The youngster watched the sweating lawyer from behind his levelled pistol. At the sight of the black muzzle pointing towards him, and the hard young features above the weapon, Rutherford sighed and shook his head.

'Please, gentlemen. No violence.' The man in the buggy wiped at his sweating face, his voice still trembling. 'I have no intention of trying to escape, you may be sure.'

'Just stay smart, an' you might live long enough to see the outside of a jail,' Anderson told him. 'Anythin' else, an' you're likely to find yourself full of holes.'

He saw the horrified shudder that his words evoked, and turned to Galvan. 'He ain't gonna be no trouble, Diego,' the dark man said. He glanced up the brush-covered slope towards the stands of timber they had just left. 'Copeland's next on our list, an' he'll be a mite harder, I reckon.'

'As you say, *amigo*.' Galvan's face showed a murderous anger at the mention of the rancher's name. 'I am anxious to meet that *hijo de la gran puta* myself. He has much to answer for.'

'You bet.' Anderson's dark Indian features, too, were grim as he answered. 'Some unfinished business of my own there, Diego.' He paused, looking to where Martin Quiroga still held the sweating Rutherford at gunpoint.

'How 'bout you have Martin take Mister Rutherford over to Teofilo's place, and keep him there until the sheriff arrives? That way, we make sure no one else gits their hands on the evidence.'

'*Bueno*,' the big Mexican nodded approvingly. His dark gaze touched on Anderson, questioning once more. 'What of Copeland?'

'We head back to the ranch-house now, we ought to find him,' Anderson said.

He took hold of the black's fallen halter-rope and stepped into his stirrup, climbing aboard. Beside him Galvan was already giving the youngster his orders. 'Martin, take this *hombre*, and go with him to the house of Señor Hernandez. Wait there until we return, to the sheriff comes. *Sabe usted?*'

'*Si*, Señor Galvan.' Martin ducked his sleek head in acknowledgement, and the big man smiled.

'Do not let him escape, Martin, and do not lose the valise. It has enough proof to free us from Copeland and his *pistoleros*.' Galvan turned his mount, urging it back towards the slope that led down the road. 'The Señor Anderson and myself will call at the Copeland ranch.'

'Señor Galvan!' Sound of the younger man's voice halted him for an instant. Galvan glanced back over his shoulder, and met the other's troubled gaze. 'Señor Galvan, there are

152

only two of you. Is this wise? Surely, when the sheriff comes...'

'No time, Martin!' Anderson cut in sharply, urging his own mount forward off the road. 'We leave Copeland too long, he'll slip out from under. Besides, we need you to watch Rutherford. *Entiende?*'

Martin frowned uncertainly, his glance moving to the grey-haired figure of Diego Galvan once again. Reading the question there, the rancher nodded. 'It is the truth, Martin,' Galvan told him. 'What is to be done must be done now, and not later.'

'As you wish, Señor Galvan.' Martin Quiroga shrugged resignedly, turning back to where Rutherford held the traces on the buggy horse. 'Turn the buggy, *hombre, muy pronto*! We go to the *casa* of Señor Hernandez.'

His sweat-stained hands slippery on the reins, Rutherford cajoled the horse to turn around, the light-wheeled vehicle following. Martin rode ahead of him, pistol held ready as they started back along the road. Behind them, Anderson and Galvan set their mounts plunging uphill through the brush, and into the trees.

'He's plannin' to call on Josefa this mornin',' Anderson said.

He spoke the words sidelong as he rode, the black horse moving sure-footedly between the trunks of the pines. Catching sight of Galvan's startled expression he grinned reassuringly,

153

shaking his head. 'Take it easy, Diego. He ain't about to move until Grierson an' Coe come back from killin' me, is he? Anyhow, I told Josefa to have the *vaqueros* armed an' ready to ride, should she need 'em. Copeland wouldn't have found it easy if he had ridden over there.' He paused, the brief grin fading as he nudged the stallion forward. 'Lucky she sent Raul an' Martin on ahead, all the same.'

'It is good to know that she is safe, Andres.' Galvan brushed the sweat from his thick, grey moustaches, guiding his mount expertly between the trees. 'How many are at the ranch-house with Copeland, my friend?'

'Three.' Anderson's face showed bleak as he answered. 'Mather, Fisher, an' Walsh Hindman. Mather's likely to be the toughest, I reckon. He wants out of this game, but he'll fight, an' there ain't many come faster with a handgun.' He glanced to the Mexican beside him, thoughtfully. 'Not even you, Diego.'

'It will be six years since I used this gun in anger,' Galvan said. He laid his hand on the butt of the .44 Griswold and Grier pistol as if to seek reassurance from the touch of the walnut wood against his palm. 'Mather has the advantage of me, to be sure, but I am an old dog to be learning new tricks, Andres. *Quien sabe?* Perhaps I have grown too old and too foolish to run from men like Lon Mather?'

'You're a good man to have along, Diego, an' that's the truth,' Anderson told him.

'All the same, Lon Mather,' the Mexican frowned, considering, 'he is a dangerous *hombre*, Andres. And with the three others ... You think we should bring along Raul and his dogs, perhaps?'

'Reckon not, *amigo*.' Anderson shook his head, the horse taking him on for the edge of the trees. 'Think it over, huh? Copeland sent two men out with me, an' he's at the ranch-house waitin' for two fellers comin' back. Two of us should make it to the house without any trouble, maybe even git the jump on them. Any more, an' they're gonna be suspicious from the start.'

'*Verdad*.' The big Mexican nodded his grizzled head, convinced. Galvan followed the dark man out of the ponderosa stand and across an open stretch into fresh timber, his hawkish face breaking to a smile. 'So, it is to be the two of us against them. This will be like the old days, my friend. And once it is over, you will be our honoured guest, after all you have done for us.'

'It ain't over yet, Diego.' Anderson entered the next cluster of trees, frowning as his keen eyes scoured the land ahead. Right now it wasn't only Lon Mather and his deadly skill with a handgun that troubled his mind. Anderson was thinking about his last meeting with Josefa, the guilt and anguish in her voice as she told him all that Diego didn't know. It would be a tough haul to come through the

155

showdown with Copeland's crew, but what came after was likely to be tougher for Galvan and Josefa, and how it would work out he had no way of knowing. 'Four *hombres* up ahead gonna want us dead, an' besides Mather, Curt Fisher's handy enough with a weapon. Copeland carries a pocket gun, an' at short range even Walsh Hindman kin hit you if he gits the chance. That's the odds, *amigo*. We've had better.'

'And worse.' Galvan still grinned, undisturbed by what he heard. 'We will take them all, Andres, and but for you I would not have had this chance.' He halted for a moment, his face grown more serious as he studied the man beside him. 'My thanks to you, *amigo*, for freeing me from that prison. I could not have borne to die with the rope around my neck.'

'It's what friends are for, Diego,' Anderson said.

He tapped heels to the stallion's sides, Galvan staying with him as they rode deeper into the pines.

*   *   *

'So where the hell is Anderson?' Tatum Hatch demanded.

He reined in to bring his mount to a halt, the riders of the posse pulling up behind him. Hatch scanned the row of faces that met him, his ruddy features hot and angry beneath a

156

sheen of dust and sweat. He'd barely made it back to Hillsburg before Josefa's messenger had arrived, and dragged him out again to get his men back on their horses. After a night spent without sleep, his temper was on a hairtrigger, especially after what he'd already heard. Now he eyed the waiting group outside Teofilo's place suspiciously, holding the Parker 10-gauge awkwardly across his saddlehorn. Wasn't only Hernandez and his family there, he saw. A buggy and a saddle horse were pulled up in front of the *casa*, and Martin Quiroga sat there grinning with a heavy valise between his feet, holding a pistol on a crestfallen Eugene Rutherford.

'He has not been here for some time, Sheriff,' the youngster told him. Seeing the stocky lawman frown as he caught sight of Rutherford, Martin nodded. '*Si*, Sheriff. This is Mister Rutherford, the lawyer who works for the Señor Copeland. He has some books and papers that will give you all the proof you are looking for, I think.'

He grinned wider, tapping the bulging case at his feet. Hatch glanced at the valise and back again to Rutherford with blue, suspicious eyes.

'Is that so?' Hatch sleeved at his sweating brow, still frowning. 'Seems to me like I better call on Mister Copeland, an' soon. Maybe we'll take a look at this stuff later, Martin. An' you best have some good answers when I do, Rutherford!'

The lawyer didn't answer, slumped with his head in his hands.

*   *   *

'Where is Anderson now, Martin?' Josefa asked.

She rode with the sheriff and Mike Riordan at the head of the posse, whose numbers were swollen by her own armed *vaqueros*. Unlike the other riders, she carried no weapon, her tall figure in its black riding-habit standing out from the rest. Meeting her eyes and the urgent query they held, Martin let the grin vanish from his face.

'He has gone to the Copeland ranch, *señora*,' the young man told her.

'Diego is with him?' Josefa's voice was more anxious than before. Again, Martin nodded.

'*Verdad, señora*.' The *vaquero* glanced to Teofilo and the others, as if seeking their agreement. 'Copeland would have murdered the Señor Anderson, but the Señor Galvan prevented it, with Raul and myself. Raul is in the timber outside the ranch, with his dogs, and has two of their men prisoner—the ones they call Grierson and Coe. Since then, we have captured Rutherford, and now they are gone for the rest.'

'*Gracias*, Martin.' Josefa spoke the words as a low, hoarse whisper. The face of the *hacendada* paled to a deathly shade, her eyes

158

huge and dark against the whiteness. Now she turned, looking pleadingly to the lawman beside her. 'Sheriff, we must follow them at once. They are in great danger.'

'That's just what I aim to do, Josefa.' Hatch swung his mount around, signing angrily to the horsemen behind him. 'Come on, you *hombres*! We got work to do!'

He set off across the open ground, urging his horse to a run. Riordan and the others moved to follow, sound of their animals' hooves clattering on the dirt and stones. Josefa halted for a moment, closing her eyes as she held tightly to the peak of her saddle.

'*Señora!*' Martin Quiroga sprang to his feet, the valise and Rutherford forgotten as he dashed towards her. Behind him the Hernandezes came running, the big sheepdogs barking beside them. '*Señnora*, you are unwell. You wish to rest, perhaps?'

Josefa recovered herself as the youngster reached her stirrup, her eyes opening as the colour returned to her face. The tall woman breathed out slowly and shook her head, warding off Martin with a lifted hand.

'It is nothing, Martin. I must go with them.' She straightened up, releasing her grip on the saddlehorn, and shook out the rein to nudge her mount forward. Josefa left the Hernandez place at a headlong gallop, plunging after the posse as the group of horsemen struck uphill into the timber, making for the ranch.

As she rode, she found herself hoping that they were not already too late.

* * *

They came to the ranch-house along the main trail that led through grassland reaching to their horses' bellies, the slopes with their ponderosa stands far behind them. Anderson and Galvan rode in through the open gateway, and up the long drive for the house itself, their mounts covering the ground at a steady, raking stride. Scanning ahead as he rode, the dark man saw the huge, Spanish-style *hacienda*, its stone walls gleaming brightly in the blaze of the risen sun, the mass of outbuildings that made an L-shape around the stone-flagged courtyard. Outside the house, his keen eyes picked out the smaller, darker figures who sighted them from a distance and now hurried into the open to meet them.

'It's them, all right.' Anderson flipped the restraining thong off the holstered .45 on his hip, hand on the gun-butt as he drove the stallion forward. 'Best be ready, *amigo*, they ain't far off now.'

Galvan didn't answer him, smiling like a hunting wolf as he eased his own pistol against the leather. Ahead of them the dark shapes grew larger, slowly taking on definition. Four men, standing in a group to await their coming. The one who led them wearing a long, dark coat that hung loosely about him.

They broke to a full gallop as they neared the sprawl of buildings, plunging headlong in for the courtyard and the men who waited. Only then, when their faces showed plainly, did recognition dawn on the bunch in the open. The four men scattered away from the oncoming riders, hunting cover as Anderson and Galvan ploughed into the yard. And, as they ran, they reached hurriedly for their holstered guns.

'*Abajo!*' Anderson yelled. He kicked from his stirrups as the black stallion knelt to his command, hurled himself clear. Stone flags of the courtyard punished him, slammed him with force enough to drive the breath out of his body for an instant. Anderson clawed out the .45 Army and rolled for the nearest of the outbuildings as the horse dropped over and lay flat to the ground. From the corner of his eye he caught a glimpse of big Walsh Hindman as the saloonman flung himself for the open door of the stables.

Mather was first to react, as he'd expected. Tall, stooping figure had his pistol from leather before the others could move, and his first shot blistered the air past Anderson's head as he dropped from the saddle. Anderson sucked in his breath as a second bullet ricocheted off the flagstones left of him with a deafening whine, then Galvan was down from his horse and shooting, the courtyard echoing to a barrage of

161

explosions as the rest of them opened up together. Next to Mather, the Mexican was quickest, beating the blond man for time as he swung towards Galvan with the Schofield lifted for a third and killing shot. Galvan triggered a split-second before him, noise of the two shots blending in a percussive rattle of sound. Heavy slug from the .44 Griswold and Grier smashed into Mather's gangling frame, hurled him backwards across the stones in an untidy sprawling tumble. Same instant Diego Galvan yelped like a kicked dog and staggered back a half-step, going down to one knee as he clasped the ragged bullet wound in his left hip.

Anderson hit against the wall of an outbuilding and raised up to a sitting position, the .45 Colt Army steadied over his left forearm as he sought for a target. Fisher was stranded in the open stretch beyond the two horses, and shooting back. Anderson heard his first try smash into *adobe* somewhere above his head, and grimaced at the vicious impact. The dark man caught sight of that pale, thin-lipped face, the snarl that distorted the gunman's features as Fisher levelled to shoot again. He pressed the trigger, felt the fierce recoil as the gun-butt hammered his palm. Force of the bullet struck Curt Fisher in the chest, spun him halfway round with his own pistol blasting flame at the ground. The sandy-haired gunhawk swayed and crashed headlong, his weapon skidding from him to ring hollowly on

162

the flags.

Anderson looked for Hindman, swore as he found no trace of the fleeing killer. The dark man coughed in the thickening reek of gunsmoke, peering through a drifting grey-blue screen that stung his eyes and made them water. He'd begun to struggle to his feet when something hit him with the power of a speeding train, and punched him into the *adobe* wall. Anderson gasped as his right shoulder went numb, the .45 Army spilling loose from his grip as he slid to the ground.

'This one's for you, breed!' Ross Copeland shouted.

The rancher loomed out of the smoke-pall towards him as he caught the shouted words. Copeland had lost his derby hat, the black Prince Albert flapping loose on his bony, angular frame. Flecks of black powder smeared the narrow face, convulsed now to a vicious mask whose eyes gleamed like glass-shards in the yellow flesh. He stumbled closer, hoisting the .44-calibre pocket pistol for a second shot, as Anderson scrabbled awkwardly to reach the captured gun in his belt. Pain seared in his wounded shoulder, and the dark man froze, gasping in shock. Anderson watched the other's pistol line on him, the narrow foxy face behind it seeming to fill the world.

Copeland never fired the shot. All at once he was staring at something over Anderson's

163

head, and reeling sideways like a drunk as the legs went from under him. Anderson saw the ugly hole appear between the rancher's eyes before the heavy concussion of the shot carried to him. Blood from the wrecked skull spattered the wall, a few drops stinging his face. Anderson gagged, tasting bile, watched as Ross Copeland went face down to the stones, already dead before he struck.

Biting his lip on the pain that scorched through his shoulder, Anderson got his left hand to the gun in his belt and tugged it free. Through the smoke he saw Diego Galvan lurch upright, staggering to stand as he pressed one hand to the wound that ran bloodily between his spread fingers. Hawkish face of the Mexican showed pale and clenched, teeth gritted as Galvan peered through the smoke towards Anderson. Behind the grey-haired man, Anderson saw Lon Mather struggle to sit up, his shirt dark with blood as he stretched for his fallen gun. Mather failed to reach the weapon, folded to collapse on his face. Closer to them, Copeland and Fisher lay without moving, their fallen bodies still as the stones beneath.

'Andres, my friend. You are hurt.' Galvan forced out the words through his teeth, his own features wracked with pain. The Mexican hobbled towards him, his pistol lowered as the sounds of gunfire died. 'Tell me they have not killed you, *amigo.*'

He crossed over to the outbuilding as Anderson gasped and tried to struggle up from the ground. And big Walsh Hindman ducked out through the door of the stable, both hands braced against the kick of the sawn-down 12-gauge Greener shot-gun as he dragged back on the double triggers.

'Diego!' Anderson's desperate yell drowned to a thunderous roar that murdered all other sound. Close-range impact of the shot-gun charge blasted Diego Galvan off his feet and hammered him into the flagstones in a flailing spatter of blood. The Mexican hit the ground with a bone-racking thud, rolled away loose and heavy as a wet sack to lie with both arms outflung, staring upwards.

The gun he'd taken from Nathan Coe was a solid-framed Remington Army. It weighed heavy as lead in his left hand as he brought the weapon painfully into line, echoes of the shot-gun blast still battering round the courtyard, and off the buildings all around. Walsh Hindman had broken the 12-gauge and was cramming fresh shells into the breech when Anderson's first shot caught him and smashed him into the doorpost like a sledgehammer on a railroad tie. The burly saloonman rebounded from the bloodstained wood, clutching the doorpost with both hands to go slowly down. Anderson's lean Indian face was stony, bare of pity. He kept tripping hammer until all the loads were gone, shot after shot crashing into the falling man to pound him down to the ground.

'No, damn it!' Anderson breathed the words aloud to the silence that rang suddenly in the wake of the gunshots. 'Goddamn it, no! Not Diego!'

He let the empty pistol fall, crawling on his knees to where Galvan lay sprawled on the bloody flagstones. Somewhere far behind him he figured he could hear the noise of hooves, and a swelling babel of voices, but right now they none of them counted. Gash in his shoulder seared like a branding-iron, turning him weak and sick, but he pushed it to some darker corner of his mind. Right now the shock he felt left no space for anything else. Anderson knelt above the fallen Mexican and grabbed him by his blood-spattered shirt, shaking Galvan fiercely with his good hand as if to rouse him awake.

'Come on, goddamn it!' the dark man shouted. He shook harder, anger and loss rising in him so strongly that he had to fight to breathe. 'For God's sake, Diego, don't die on me now!'

In his grasp the body of his friend lolled, slack and unresponsive, the hawkish face and its dark eyes fixed in a savage, startled glare. Below the chest, Diego's body had all but disappeared, blasted and torn by the buckshot to a mass of bloody flesh. He hugged the dead man closer, and the head lolled against him, the eyes staring emptily through him to some other far-off place.

He heard the harsh, racking sound of someone weeping, out of control. Taste of tears on his face told Anderson the sound came from him, and the sudden awareness shocked him. He hadn't shed tears over anyone since he was a boy. Murderous anger replaced the grief, and he snarled at the figures who came forward to help him. Sight of Hatch and Riordan and the others fuelled his rage, and he lashed out at them, warning them off with what little strength was left him. Didn't the bastards know they were too late?

They hadn't hanged Galvan, after all. But in the end it made no difference.

Through the looming mass around him he saw Josefa come forward, felt the silence fall like a world ending as she halted by him. The face of the tall woman showed numbed and pale, shocked out of feeling for the moment. Anderson forced himself to meet her stricken gaze, cradling the grey head of Galvan on his lap as he felt the strength run out of him faster than grain from a ripped sack.

'Josefa, I'm sorry.' Seemed like it took him a mind-sapping effort to speak the words. Anderson peered uncertainly as the faces clouded to darkness around him. 'Maybe I could have saved him, but I had to use the left hand ... I was way too slow, Josefa.'

Josefa didn't speak, her pale face still frozen

167

in shock. Then he heard her scream. The noise was unbearable, a terrible bereaved howling that ripped the silence jaggedly open. Anderson felt that scream shiver through him, and the darkness all around caved and showered down to bury him like a collapsing mineshaft, smothering his face until he could no longer breathe.

After that, he quit trying to remember.

CHAPTER NINE

He stood beside Josefa as the last spadefuls of dirt were flung into the open grave, and waited for the mourners who now filed back to meet them. Anderson saw the earth cover the coffin that held the body of Diego Galvan, made his own goodbyes in silence. He stayed quiet as Josefa shook hands with Hatch and Mike Riordan, and the others who'd come along, his own glance cutting downslope from the graveyard with its shading *piñons* to the *adobe* sprawl of Hillsburg far below. At least some good ought to come from it, he figured. Even if it wasn't too easy to understand right now.

'Sure wish we didn't none of us have to be here, Josefa.' Hatch's ruddy face sweated in the heat, its sorrowful expression matching the stumbling of his words. The stocky lawman pressed her hands, let them go awkwardly.

'You take care of yourself, now, you hear?'

'It seems that I must, Mister Hatch.' Josefa's smile was shaky and uncertain. In the light of morning her features showed pale, but the red-rimmed eyes were dry. Diego's widow had done her crying long before, and now only the emptiness of loss remained. That, and the pride that would have to sustain her in the times to come. 'You were kind to be here today, yourself and the Señor Riordan. For this, you have my thanks.'

'Wasn't nothin'',' Riordan told her. 'Diego was a good man, one of the best. Least we could do was see him buried decent.'

Josefa nodded, struggling to hold on to her smile. Hatch and Mike moved on to Anderson, who shook with them carefully, left-handed. Surface gash that scarred the right shoulder was halfway healed by now, but the arm still handled stiffly, and he guessed it would take time to mend.

'Don't look like you need worry, come election time,' he told the sheriff, and Hatch nodded, shrugging his burly shoulders.

'No problems from Copeland, that's for sure,' the stocky lawman agreed. 'Syndicate back in Chicago got their fingers burned, an' they'll lie low for a while, I reckon.' Hatch slapped the hat on his balding skull, starting uphill from the graveyard. 'Be seein' you, Anderson.'

'You too, Hatch.' Anderson shook hands

with the lanky Riordan. 'No hard feelings, Mike?'

'Reckon not.' The horsy-faced deputy shook his head. 'Safe journey, feller.'

He followed Hatch upslope through the trees, his bony shoulders hunched as he climbed. Anderson exchanged farewells with Teofilo and his family, and watched them leave. Pretty soon the graveyard was empty but for himself and Josefa, and Raul and Martin, who stood some yards away in the *piñon* shade, the oldster keeping his two restless mastiffs on their leash.

'Now it is over, Andres,' Josefa said.

He didn't answer her for a while, studying the ground by his feet. Sure, it was over, one way at least. Copeland, Fisher and Hindman were dead. Mather, it seemed would live to stand trial, and would most likely get a prison term, along with Coe, and Grierson, and Rutherford. Compared with Diego, Mather had been lucky. Even if he was unlikely to come out to jail the same man he'd been before.

Another way, it wasn't over at all. It was the start of a long, hard road, and Josefa would have to take it alone. Not only without Diego, the husband they'd clear of murder now it was too late, but her lover Espinoza. He hadn't said too much to her about the foreman since Diego died. Josefa would find out soon enough, if she didn't know already. Now, from alongside, her voice reached for him again.

170

'Andres, do not blame yourself.' She came over, laying a hand on his good arm, gentleness and sadness mingled in her look. 'You did all that you could. No man could have done more.'

'Maybe.' Anderson didn't sound too sure. He tried for a smile of his own, couldn't quite make it. 'Looks like you're about to become a wealthy woman, anyhow, sittin' on them minerals they been talkin' about. Ranchin' or minin', reckon it's up to you.'

'Presently I will decide.' Josefa shrugged off the thought, her face grown more serious. 'For now, there is something else you must know. Doctor Kelly tells me there will be a child, in the spring.'

'Uhuh.' Anderson turned that one over for a while, nodded at last. 'Couldn't have a better ma, an' that's the truth.'

'*Gracias*, Andres.' He heard the faint quiver in her voice, caught the tremulous smile. 'You were always the best of our friends.'

'So now you're a *segundo* short, huh?'

At once, she shook her head. 'No, Andres.' Josefa's tone brightened, and she glanced to the two waiting men in the shade of the trees. 'We shall need a new *vaquero*. Martin will act as *segundo*.'

'Is that right?' Anderson followed her gaze, catching the young Mexican's eager nod, the more knowing smile of Raul Nunez. 'Well, if that don't beat all.'

171

'You will stay with us for a while,' Josefa was saying. The *hacendada* clasped his hands firmly, her voice entreating. 'For a few days at least, until you are fit to ride. You will be welcome, you know this.'

'Sure, I know it.' Anderson sounded almost as tired as he felt. Meeting her eyes, the dark man shook his head. 'Reckon not, Josefa. Shoulder's all but healed, figure it won't give me no trouble. An' I got a town back there in Old Mexico. Thanks for the offer, but it's time I went back.' He returned the grip of her hands, starting to smile. 'Just take real good care of yourself, OK? I'll be back.'

'*Vaya con Dios*, Andres.' He saw her chin lift in that familiar, determined way of hers as she answered, and knew she'd make it. Wealthy or not, the next few months would be tougher on Josefa than anyone else, but like he'd told Diego she was one hell of a woman. If anyone could come through it, she was the one.

'You too, Josefa.' He gripped her hands, and released them. Anderson shook with Raul and Martin, and headed up the slope to where his horse stood tethered in the shade. Halting to untie the stallion's rope, he glanced back a last time to the fresh-dug grave and its crude wooden cross.

Sorry, Diego, he told the silent mound of earth. I did my best. Too bad it didn't work out the way it should.

In its swathe of bandages the right shoulder

protested, nagging him with a dull, persistent ache as he climbed into the saddle. Walking the black away from the graveyard, answering their waves, the dark man ignored the discomfort. This moment, he reckoned it didn't matter.

It was another kind of wound he carried with him out of Hillsburg, and one that would take a longer time to heal.

We hope you have enjoyed this Large Print book. Other Chivers Press or G.K. Hall Large Print books are available at your library or directly from the publishers. For more information about current and forthcoming titles, please call or write, without obligation, to:

Chivers Press Limited
Windsor Bridge Road
Bath BA2 3AX
England
Tel. (01225) 335336

OR

G.K. Hall
P.O. Box 159
Thorndike, Maine 04986
USA
Tel. (800) 223–2336

All our Large Print titles are designed for easy reading, and all our books are made to last.